POUNDING EARTH

STARCROSSED DRAGONS BOOK 4

ERIN BEDFORD

J. A. CIPRIANO

WANT TO GET FREE STUFF?

<u>Sign up here.</u> If you do, I'll send you some free short stories.

Visit Erin on Facebook or on the web at ErinBedford.com.

<u>The Celestial War Chronicles</u>

Song of Blood and Fire

Visions of War and Water

<u>The Mary Wiles Chronicles</u>

Marked By Hell

Bound By Hell

Deceived By Hell

Tempted By Hell

<u>The Crimson Fold</u>

Until Midnight

Vampire CEO

Granting Her Wish

ALSO BY J.A. CIPRIANO

<u>Starcrossed Dragons</u>

Riding Lightning

Grinding Frost

Swallowing Fire

Pounding Earth

<u>The Goddess Harem</u>

The Tiger's Offer

The Wolf's Hunt

The Dragon's War

<u>Justice Squad</u>

Miracle's Touch

<u>Her Angels</u>

Heaven's Embrace

Heaven's A Beach

Heaven's Most Wanted

The Shaman Queen's Harem

Ghosts and Grudges

1

———

"Oooh, right there," I moaned, leaning into Raiden's touch. His fingers dug into my shoulders, hitting just the right spot to make me squirm. I'd been waiting all day for this moment. The moment I would get to finally relax and sink my aching body into the bath tub. Raiden joining me had been a bonus.

"Like that, do you?" Raiden chuckled in my ear, making the water slosh around us. We'd taken refuge in my bathroom after spending all day in the training field. The North might be a frozen icy land, but they did have some killer training grounds.

"You have no idea." I groaned again and shifted closer to him. "I'm happy you guys are helping me get stronger, but it's killer on my muscles."

"You shouldn't overwork yourself." Raiden turned me slightly to look at him. "You're still pregnant."

"So?" I arched a brow. "I'm pregnant, not weak." I stroked my hand along my swelling belly. My second trimester had begun, and our daughter had done her best to make herself known. One day, I was staring down at a flat stomach, and the next thing I know, my belly button was several inches further out than it had been before.

It didn't bother me, really. I wasn't vain. Living with my father had taught me to have a tough skin and to accept myself the way I was born. In fact, the more my daughter grew, the less I cared about what I looked like, and the more I worried about getting stronger.

I couldn't rely on the guys to keep me safe every minute of every day. There were too many enemies, and more being added by the day. The only people not trying to kill us were Firestar's family. Though that might change if they ever figured out that we had lied about Firestar being my only mate.

"What's wrong?" Raiden asked, dropping his hands from my shoulders.

I shrugged but didn't answer.

Not accepting my silence, Raiden turned me in

his arms so that I sat curled up on his muscular front. He brushed his thumb against the side of my face, pushing a stray wet hair away.

"Is it the baby?" The concern in his eyes made my heart warm more than I could handle. The guys had been so loving toward me, and that love had grown the farther along I got in my pregnancy. I partly suspected it was my unbalanced hormones that made them act so caring, but since I'd started to level out a bit more, they hadn't let up.

"No, she's fine." I smiled, placing my hand on my stomach. "Getting hungry but fine."

"Then what is it."

"Aren't you worried?" I finally asked, shifting so that I could sit more comfortably in his lap.

"About the baby?" Raiden raised a brow, and I shook my head.

I chewed on my bottom lip as I tried to find a delicate way to bring up his mother and father. Raiden hadn't gotten better at hearing about the mother that betrayed him and his family, so I didn't want to poke at him more than needed.

"Come now." Raiden gave me his trademark grin. "There's nothing you can't tell me, Maya. I love you. Nothing you could say would change that."

Tell that to his mother.

Lady Nariko had all but obliterated her family with her lust for power. The moment she found out that I could give powers to my lovers, she had turned into a power-hungry monster. It wasn't enough that her youngest son was benefiting from my powers, she needed all her sons to be the strongest.

Her sons and husband didn't share the same opinion, and sadly, that led to Lady Nariko to stage a coup. She had thrown Lord Shen, Raiden's father, into the dungeon and had tried to do the same to her sons. Fortunately, Raiden's twin brothers were safe here with us in the North, but we didn't know if Lord Shen was still alive.

Unable to hesitate any longer, I asked, "Do you think your father is okay?"

Raiden's grin wilted on the edges, and then it came back in full force. "Oh, I'm sure of it. We Easterners are survivors. How else do you think I would have lived through my brothers growing up?" He laughed, but it was forced.

I couldn't imagine how Raiden was feeling, what he had pent up inside of him. My relationship with my family had always been shaky, so I'd never had the close-knit, loving kind of bonds Raiden had with his. And for his mother to betray them all like that? Unbelievable. I would expect it from my father. He only had his own well-being in mind. But the heartbreaking way Raiden and his brothers looked when they found out their mother was not the person they knew? My own heart ached for them.

Now, all I could do was be there for him and help him save his father and his kingdom. For him and for our daughter.

"Do you think we'll make a move soon?" I asked, running a hand through his black and white hair. He leaned into my touch, his eyes closing briefly. When they opened, they were hard.

"If we don't soon, we are going to lose the few warriors we have."

Things were getting tense around the Northern kingdom. The warriors we had procured for Raiden's father's rescue wanted to know when we would get started, something I wanted to know as well.

"Do you think we have a chance with the men we have?" I asked though I knew the answer.

Raiden sighed. "If we attack now, we'd be committing suicide." He shook his head, making me drop my hand. "We are better off waiting for more supporters, but where we'll get them, I have no idea."

I slid closer to him, pressing myself against him as much as my belly would let me. "We'll save him, Raiden," I assured him, hoping my eyes showed the confidence I was faking. "We won't let your mother win."

"I know." Raiden gave me a small smile, his arms wrapping around my waist. He drew me down for a soft kiss which ended sooner than I would have liked. "You just take care of yourself and our daughter and leave the worrying to us. After all, why else would you need three men?"

I smirked. "Oh, I know a few reasons."

"Is that right?" Raiden leered at me, his hands moving up against my back. I could feel him growing beneath me, and it made me wiggle slightly. Raiden groaned and cupped my butt, grinding his erection against me.

Placing my hands on his shoulders, I rubbed myself against his length. Hot sparks of need shot through me, making my insides clench. One benefit of this pregnancy had been the increasing aware-ness of every nerve ending in my body. Just one slight vibration could have me orgasming on the spot. Helpful in the bedroom, not so much when in the middle of training.

Slick and hungry for more friction, I lifted myself up. Reaching between us, Raiden aligned himself with my wet folds. Even without any foreplay, I was still more than ready for him, but each inch I sank onto him stretched and rubbed me until I sighed in pleasure.

Swallowing hard, I enjoyed the feel of him inside of me for just a moment. Raiden didn't move, his eyes trained on my face. I licked my lips and nodded when I'd had my fill.

Hands on my hips, he lifted me gently. My head fell back at the sensation and a low gurgling groan released from my throat. Every nerve jolted as if they had downed five cans of Red Bull. I chuckled slightly at the thought. My best friend Ryan from Earth would be appalled to know I had used his favorite drink as a sex reference.

"Laughter is not usually the reaction I'm going for when I'm inside of you," Raiden reminded me, and I smiled down at him.

"Sorry, just had a funny thought."

He quirked a brow. "Well, do tell," I opened my mouth to do so, but he tweaked my nipple, making me yip. "Later. Tell me later. After I've thoroughly fucked you into oblivion."

"So sure of yourself, are you?" I quipped and then groaned as he moved me along his length again. My fingernails dug into his shoulders, and I gasped.

Raiden grinned. "Yes, I am."

Panting, I said, "Less talking, more moving."

"Yes, ma'am." Raiden thrust up into me, hitting the back of me with a sharp sting. I'd once worried our aggressive lovemaking might hurt the baby, but Trina had assured us that as long as we weren't doing anything too extreme, she'd be fine. She was a dragon after all. Aggression was kind of our calling card.

Letting me control our movements for a while, Raiden cupped my breasts in his hands. They felt heavy even with Raiden holding them. He rolled the sensitive peaks in between his fingers, sending electric pangs of pleasure through me. I rotated my hips against him, clenching my walls around his length. Raiden paused in his ministrations to let out a heavy groan.

"You don't play fair," he accused, thrusting up into me with more force. Gripping his hair in my hands, I buried my face into his neck. I sought out the pulsing vein along the junction of his throat and skimmed my teeth against it.

The reaction was instant. Suddenly, I was lifted out of his lap and turned to face the edge of the tub. I gripped the side of the tub, my breasts now fully out of the water causing my nipples to harden tightly. I propped my knees up on the small ledge beneath the water's surface, putting my ass up in the air.

"You're going to pay for that," Raiden growled, his fingers tangling in my dark tresses. He tugged on them slightly, arching my head back. His other hand moved slowly over the swell of my hip, teasing and taunting me.

"Please," I gasped as his fingers dipped in between my thighs. As if he hadn't heard me, Raiden kept moving in his own way, barely caressing my bundle of nerves before dipping inside of my entrance, none of the actions giving me much relief.

"I'm not sure you really want it." Raiden's length bumped against my butt. "You seem more interested playing around."

"No," I gasped just as he moved his fingers back to my clit. "I promise to behave."

"Oh?" Raiden cooed. "So, you didn't bite me? I

thought you were aware of who held the control in this relationship."

God damn him and his need for control. I had bitten him but not as a show of dominance. I just wanted him to get a move on. When you are constantly on the brink of orgasm, a girl could only take so much. If I had done the same thing to Jack or Firestar, they would have taken the hint and pounded into me until I was a pile of goo.

Not Raiden.

I wasn't sure if it was because he was the youngest of three boys or if that was just the way he was wired, but Raiden always needed to prove something to me. It was funny, really. Out of the bedroom, I could boss him around, and he didn't say anything. But behind closed doors, he needed me begging and pleading for my release.

Not that I was complaining. He made me work for it sure, but it was worth it. Every knee shaking, teeth clenching moment of it.

So, I gave him what he wanted, and he gave me what I needed. A good fucking and a mind-blowing orgasm. Win-win.

"You're in charge," I bit out and pushed my ass into him. "Please, Raiden. I need …"

"What do you need?" he asked, a demanding tone in his voice that made me gush down low.

"You."

"Be more specific, pet." Raiden removed his fingers from me, and I let out a keening moan. "You know what I want to hear, Maya."

The way he said my name did it for me. Like a delectable dessert, he wanted to gobble me up if only I would give him permission. Cause that's what this was all really about. My permission. My surrender. I had to surrender myself to him, and he would take care of me. In all ways.

"I want you to fuck me." I snapped, my patience growing thin at the play. I could blame my pregnancy, but really, I only wanted to be teased so much before I got grumpy.

"Ah," Raiden purred. "That's what I wanted to hear." Releasing my hair, he spread my nether lips before positioning himself back at my entrance. Before I could take a breath, he sheathed himself inside of me.

He didn't give me any warning as he thrust into me at a rapid pace. My breath came out in pants, and my fingers gripped the side of the tub so hard, I worried I might break it. I didn't bother to hold back my cries of pleasure, I knew he'd want to hear them.

"That's it, pet," Raiden encouraged me as I moaned loudly. "Tell me just what you want."

I closed my eyes tightly as my orgasm approached. It was almost there when a noise made my eyes shoot open. Firestar stood in the doorway of the bathroom, his arms crossed over his chest and his eyes hot. Raiden didn't stop moving, nor did shy away from Firestar's gaze.

With my eyes locked with his, I was just this shy of orgasming when Raiden pulled me away from the side of the tub. My hands instantly went behind me to hold on to him as he arranged me in his lap. My legs straddled his, my back to his front giving Firestar a full view of my body and Raiden's length moving inside of me.

"Isn't she beautiful?" Raiden asked Firestar, one hand cupping my breast while the other held me in place. I knew what he was doing. Firestar was the most territorial of all my men. Jack and Raiden shared well, which they had proved to me on more than one occasion. Firestar not so much.

Grunting, Firestar didn't answer but did take a step closer.

The hand on my hip slid between my lips and

rubbed my clit. I finally broke. The combination of Raiden's ministrations and Firestar's attention was too much for me. My head fell back against Raiden, and I cried out, my hands grabbing at whatever I could find, which ended up being Raiden's hair.

If I was hurting him he didn't complain, nor did he stop moving inside of me. Firestar was now at the edge of the tub, his hands tightening on his biceps. Why he forced himself back, I didn't know but had a feeling that it wouldn't last for much longer.

Raiden thrust into me a few more time before he stilled, a shaky groan coming from him. Shifting me to the side, he kissed the side of my neck. "See? Beautiful."

Sagging in his arms, I didn't even have the energy to reprimand him. Teasing Firestar had been Raiden's hobby, but now I had a feeling that it might be more than that. Maybe he was trying to make the alpha male lighten up some. Firestar could be a bit intense at times.

Instead of answering Raiden, Firestar offered me a hand. Taking it, I allowed him to towel me off. I had to hold onto him for the most part, my legs were still too shaky to stand on their own.

"The meeting will be starting soon," Firestar

announced after he was finished. "You should get ready if you want to attend."

The never-ending debate on what to do next would finally be answered tonight. Me, my men, Jack's Uncle, and the head of the three tribes who had agreed to help would meet to discuss tactics. I hoped it meant we would stop waiting. Not that I didn't enjoy spending more time with my men, but the waiting wasn't putting up any closer to saving Lord Shen or easing Raiden's worry.

"Sorry, we took a bit longer than intended." I wrapped the towel around myself and tried to look contrite. When Firestar rolled his eyes, I knew I'd failed.

"I blame it on Raiden."

"Hey!" Raiden protested jumping from the tub. Water dripped down his deliciously muscular body and my libido flared up with renewed need. I was a lucky, lucky girl.

"It wasn't all him." I agreed, turning my hungry gaze from Raiden reluctantly. "Besides, don't pretend like you wouldn't have done the same."

Firestar's lips ticked up slightly. "Just get ready."

He stalked from the room, and Raiden called out after him, "I guess I'll just dry myself off, thanks!"

2

"What do you think will happen?" I whispered to Raiden as we made our way to Jack's Uncle Fafnir's office. The Northern Lord had been more than a gracious host. Giving us sanctuary when everyone else was out to get us. Even my own home wasn't safe, not with my cousin Ned there.

Raiden squeezed my hand. "It'll be fine. These are seasoned warriors, not some group of squabbling children."

A shout and crash came from ahead of us. Quickening our pace, we rushed to the office door. Raiden shoved the door open to see Firestar pinning one of the tribe leaders against the wall.

"I stand corrected." Raiden shook his head.

The other two tribe leaders jumped to their feet, but Lord Fafnir waved them off and sat back down himself. Firestar growled lowly to the man, too quietly for me to make out what he was saying, but if I knew Firestar, he wasn't asking him to be best buds.

I sighed dramatically, causing Jack, sitting in a chair off to the side, to glance my way. His pale eyes focused on me as he stood, and I didn't even pretend that I wasn't eating him up with my eyes.

Jack was a delicious specimen in and out of clothes. He'd give any GQ model a run for their money the way his suit jacket stretched across his broad shoulders and tapered at his waist. He had left his long white hair loose, and it fell down his back in a cascade of silk.

I'd had those strands trailing down my body as he moved inside of me. Just seeing them caused my lower half to clench in need. When Jack stopped before me, I arched up on my tip toes and pressed my lips to his cool ones. His hand curved along my hip, bringing me flush against him.

It was an unusual amount of touching for a public place for him. I didn't complain though. Ever since he had cast Gretchen, his ex, aside in front of everyone, he had been purposely more affectionate, like he had something to prove. Which I suppose he did. Ever since we got to the North, he had made one screw up after another, but he had been trying his best to make amends. I couldn't fault him for that.

He might be the father of my child after all.

Pulling away from the kiss, I nodded toward Firestar who had finally let the guy go. "What's his problem?"

Jack frowned and turned toward our fourth. "Rick called Firestar a hot head for suggesting we attack head on."

"And his way of disproving that is to attack him?" Raiden asked with a grin. "Like a hot head?"

"He had it coming," Firestar answered, coming over to us. His auburn hair was tousled from running his hands through it too many times. His brown eyes narrowed as he glanced over his shoulder at Rick, the leader he had attacked. "Guy doesn't know what he's talking about."

"Or you're just a hot head." Raiden countered and ducked just in time to miss Firestar's fist. "Temper, temper." Raiden clucked and shook his head.

I placed a hand on Firestar's chest, the thick muscle beneath it twitching in response. "Please, boys, play nice. We have enough going on without having to play referee in your squabbles." I eyeballed Raiden, who gave me a cheeky grin.

A throat cleared, and we turned our attention to Lord Fafnir. He sat behind his desk, his hands laced in front of him, an impatient frown on his lips. "Maya, I'm happy to see you are doing well. How is my grandchild?"

Shifting in place, I forced a smile. "She's fine."

"Good." He gave a curt nod. "Then can we get to work here?" Lord Fafnir gestured his head toward the other waiting leaders.

Properly chastised, we moved further into the room. Jack led me to his seat, and the three of them stood behind me like a protective force. I felt kind of silly, like I was the most important person in the room. To my guys, I supposed I was. Or I just had a big head.

"So," Lord Fafnir started, his eyes going back to the three leaders. "As we were discussing before, a direct attack would not be beneficial to anyone—"

"If we go in like I—" Firestar started at my left shoulder.

"That would be suicide," Rick cut in, making Firestar step toward him. I grabbed hold of his arm, giving him pause.

"Enough." Both Rick and Firestar glared at

Lord Fafnir but quieted. "I will not have a brawl in my office. We are civilized men, let's act like it."

"Speak for yourself," Raiden muttered to my right. I shot him a warning look, and he winked, laughter in his eyes.

"No offense, my lord," Dreds, one of the other tribe leaders, began. "But I don't understand why you allow these foreigners to be in this discussion."

Firestar growled, "We have every right to be here, as much as you do."

Dreds locked eyes with Firestar. "I'm just saying, these are our men we are committing to the young lord's cause. We should be the ones deciding how they should be used."

I didn't know if it was the young lord comment or maybe Raiden was just being himself, but his next words couldn't be considered anything other than hostile.

"It's this young lord's family and people who are in danger, and he wants the only people he can trust to be in this room." Raiden shifted forward slightly, his body tensing beside me. "If you don't like it, then maybe we don't need your men after all."

"Maybe you don't." Dreds countered with a frown.

"Now, hold on a moment." Jack finally entered

the conversation. "Let's not let our emotions cloud our judgment. Dreds is right to be concerned for his men, as much as you are right to be concerned for your family, Raiden, but we all want the same thing here, to take back the east." He paused and glanced around the room and, when no one objected, continued, "Leaving Lady Nariko on the throne would not be beneficial to anyone. Not with how she's already made changes."

"Changes?" I twisted in my seat to look at Jack. "What do you mean?"

Jack looked down at me a reluctant look in his eyes. "We just got word from some of the twins' men on the inside that Lady Nariko has ordered a curfew on the people, limiting the market to being open for a very limited time each day, as well as banning any public gatherings of more than three people."

"Afraid of a revolt, I'm sure." Raiden huffed. "My mother was always the suspicious type. Though she has right to be now." He chuckled bitterly.

"What about her friend?" Lord Fafnir asked. "Is Drac still holding the border?"

Nodding, Jack placed a hand on my shoulder. "A bunch of cutthroats and pirates. The few scouts we'd sent out to check the situation barely made it out alive, some not at all."

"Should she be in here while we talk about this?" Deric gestured toward me with a concerned look. "It might be a bit … unpleasant for a woman in her condition."

Anger rage through me like an inferno. My hands gripped the edges of my chair as I leaned forward. "Are you implying that being pregnant means I no longer have a brain?"

"No, of course not." Deric tried to backtrack. "I'm just saying—"

"What?" I snapped, my face heating until I felt almost feverish. "That I'm feeble and too delicate to hear the horrors of what my mother in law has done?"

Deric tried to argue again, but I didn't give him a chance.

"I would think that I should have some say in all this since it all started with me. I should be the one to end it, don't you think?" My voice rose to a shout, and even Firestar placed a hand on my arm, but I jerked it away. The heat spread now from my face to my arms and torso, as my anger grew exponentially.

"Maya." Firestar's low rumble pulled my

burning gaze from the ice dragon. "You're burning up, and that's saying something coming from me."

I glanced up at Firestar. "I'm fine." But even I knew that was a lie. I'd never felt such a sudden fever come over me before, and I couldn't stop it. The fiery rage filled me until I felt as if I might explode at any moment.

"Maya?" This time it was Jack who said my name. The cool sound of his voice usually calmed me but, in this case, only irritated me further.

"I said, I'm fine," I shouted, turning in my seat to shove at him. At first, I wasn't sure what had happened. One minute, Jack was standing there full of concern and the next he was slammed against the back wall, his jacket on fire.

Shouts filled my ears as the ice dragons rushed to his side, using their magic to put out the flame. Horrified at what I'd done, I stared down at my hand with wide eyes and then back to Jack. I'd done that. That fire had come from me.

"Maya?" Raiden's hesitant voice barely registered in my ear. I glanced to the side where his hand hovered in mid-air as if afraid to touch me.

A large warm hand landed on my arm, and my attention turned to Firestar. "You're not hot anymore."

The statement made me realize he was right. The heat, the burning feeling had disappeared the moment I'd hit Jack. But what had caused it to begin with?

"See?" Deric scoffed from Jack's side. "She doesn't need to be in here if she can't control her own magic."

"It's not my magic," I snapped and then slowly said, "I think it's the baby's." My eyes went to Firestar as I realized what the fireball meant. I didn't have control over fire. I could control plants and do basic spells all dragons could use, like levitation, but fire? That wasn't in my wheel house. But it was in Firestar's.

Firestar's mouth dropped open at my implication, and then a proud sort of grin covered his lips.

"Great." Raiden snorted. "Now, he's going to get a big head."

"You would too." Firestar's gaze snapped to Raiden's.

"Damn straight I would." Raiden brushed his thumb against his nose and chuckled.

"Don't worry, I'm fine," Jack snarked from the wall. My eyes shot back over to him, where he had proceeded to remove his ruined jacket and shirt. The pale, muscular expanse of his skin was unmarred by the flames. I licked my lips. I would never get enough of looking at my guys. I'd never figure out how I'd gotten so lucky.

"Stop looking at me like that, love," Jack commanded, and I shook my head, clearing the lust from my face.

"Are you sure you're alright?" I asked, suddenly feeling guilty about drooling over him when I'd just thrown him across the room.

"Yes," Jack answered, coming closer to me so I could inspect him. "Just a bit of bruising and a ruined suit. I liked that one by the way." The amusement in his eyes wasn't lost on me, and I grinned.

"I'll make it up to you."

"I'm sure you will." Jack smiled slightly and traced my lips with his fingertip. "But now we have more pressing matters."

"Oh, yeah. The attack." I nodded in agreement.

"No, pet." Raiden urged me to stand up. "He's talking about you."

"What?" I glanced at the guys. "I'm fine now. I swear."

Firestar shook his head. "That might be the case, but I have to agree with Deric on this one. If you're channeling our child's abilities, anything that upsets you might be a hazard to anyone in this room."

I chewed on my lip. He had a point. I didn't want to set our host on fire because he said something I didn't like. Or the guys. Crap. Did that mean I'd have to stay away from everyone but Firestar? How would that work? Man, my head hurt.

Sighing in defeat, I threw my hands up. "Fine. I guess I'll just go to my room or something."

"Or," Jack interjected before I could get to the door, "you could go to see Trina. Make sure everything is alright?"

Nodding, I placed my hand on the door handle. "Sure. Good idea. I'll do that." I paused before opening the door. "You'll fill me in later, right?"

"Of course." Lord Fafnir answered a serious expression on his face. "Just take care of yourself and please try not to burn down my house. It took centuries to get it right."

With a nervous chuckle, I darted out of the room. I had a feeling burning down the house would be the least of my worries. What am I going to do when I go into labor?

3

On the way to the infirmary, my insides were numb. I still couldn't believe what had happened.

I'd shot a fireball out of my hand! Out of all the things I'd expected from this pregnancy, that was not one of them.

Glancing down at my stomach, I raised a brow. "Any more surprises you want to drop on me?" When she didn't respond, I sighed and kept heading to the infirmary.

Pushing the door open, I searched around for Trina, the head medic. I found her white head of hair bent over a patient, muttering some soothing words to a young man. From here, it looked like he'd broken his arm.

I cleared my throat a few feet away from the end of his bed. Trina glanced up from the young man and held up a finger. I nodded and turned my gaze away from them giving him some privacy.

When she was done Trina approached me. "Hello, Maya. How are you? Good?"

I laced my fingers in front of me and rocked on my heels. "Besides, shooting fireballs out of my hand? Sure. Peachy."

Trina's eyes widened and then she smoothed her face over. Clearing her throat, she looked down at her clipboard. "And I'm assuming that's not normal?"

"Not for an earth dragon, no." I offered her a small smile. "We think it might be something to do with the baby."

"So, you believe you may be channeling her powers?" Trina's brow rose, and then she hummed. "That's possible. It's not entirely unheard of." She started toward the back, and I assumed she meant for me to follow.

"Why did you come down here by yourself?" Trina asked with a disapproving look. "I would think one of your men would want to be here for you. Especially after something as scary as a new power."

I shrugged. "I hadn't thought about it at the time. Still, a bit shocked it happened really. Plus, there was the whole meeting going on about what to do with the East. I figure getting things moving there is probably more important than my little surprise."

"Never."

I turned, shocked to see Firestar standing in the doorway. Something tight inside of me relaxed. I hadn't realized how freaked out I'd been. Without a word, I moved into his embrace letting his arms wrap around me. I inhaled deeply, loving the wood smoke scent that was distinctively his.

"Thank you for being here," I murmured into his chest, squeezing him tightly.

"Even though it took us a second to realize we shouldn't have let you go along?"

I smiled up at him. "Even so. You're here now."

"Yes, you are." Trina sat her clipboard down with a loud clack. "And if you don't mind, I have other patients to see so …?" She gestured for me to get on the examining table.

Releasing Firestar, I moved onto the table and laid back. Firestar stepped up next to me and took my hand. I met his gaze, tightening my grasp in his.

Trina lifted my shirt up, exposing my swollen

stomach. She held her hand over my stomach, a soft glow coming from her palm. Instantly, I heard the heartbeat coming from my stomach. It made my throat clog up, and I swallowed thickly.

Trying to force back my hormonal need to cry, I watched Trina's face. Her brow furrowed tightly, and she cocked her head to the side.

"What is it?" I leaned up on my elbows. "Is the baby okay?"

Trina jerked as if startled and then shook her head with a smile. "Don't worry, your babies are fine."

I sighed and laid back on the table before jerking up again. "Wait, what'd you say?"

Grinning like a mad woman, Trina said, "You heard me right. Babies, plural."

My mouth fell open, and I glanced at Firestar who looked just as shocked. I turned my attention back to Trina, who seemed highly amused. "Are you sure?"

"Listen again." She placed her hands back on my stomach, and the heartbeat sounded in my ears.

This time though, I focused on it harder. I shook my head. "I only hear one heartbeat."

"Oh," Trina cried and then adjusted her hands. "Your babies are so in tune with each other that it's hard to pick one heartbeat out from the other. That's why I didn't catch it until now. I should be able to separate it enough for you to hear them."

I waited and listened. The one heartbeat slowly became two … and then three. If my eyes weren't wide before they had to look like giant baseballs now. I grabbed Firestar's hand harder, my own heartbeat pounding in my chest.

"What is it?" Firestar asked, worry etching his face. "What's wrong?"

"Three," I muttered.

"What?"

I coughed and shook my head to clear it. "There's three heartbeats, Firestar. Three!"

Firestar's face paled, and I gripped his hand tighter. "Don't you pass out on me." Firestar nodded and took a deep breath.

"I'm good." He licked his lips and swallowed, nodding again. "I'm not going to pass out."

Reassured that I wouldn't have to worry about Firestar collapsing on me, I turned back to Trina. "So, what does this mean?"

Clicking her tongue, Trina tucked her hands into the pockets of her pants. "I'd say that you should expect a few more surprises to come your way."

"More surprises?" I arched a brow. "I'm not sure I can handle any more surprises."

Trina chuckled. "I'm afraid that's not how this works. Babies have a mind of their own, I should know. I have four."

"Four!" I gasped.

"Believe me, triplets will be much harder for you than my four. I, at least, had time to practice with the first one before the next three came along. You'll have them all at once." I must have had a terrified look on my face because she patted me on the hand. "Don't worry. Three against four?" she glanced at Firestar with a smile. "I think you can handle it."

"Handle what?"

The three of us turned to see Raijin and Fujin pushing back the curtain of the back area. If I didn't know any better, I'd have said Raiden and the twins were actually triplets. From their strong jawlines to the almost pitch-black color of their eyes, down to the 'can't be serious if their lives depended on it' attitudes, the three sons of Lord Shen were carbon copies of each other. Even Lord Shen had the same semblance despite his age.

Most people would need the difference in hair-styles to tell the difference between them. I didn't.

Fujin might have short hair, but he also had a shorter temper and didn't smile as often as Raijin. I didn't need my eyes to tell the difference between Raiden and his brothers. Just the smell of him alone set my body on fire, something his twins didn't do.

In fact, since the seer's vision, I'd felt nothing but awkward around the twins. "You have more room in your heart," was what she said.

I'd automatically thought the twins were who she meant, especially since they were the ones that found me, but the more time around them I spent the less likely that seemed true. And now this with the babies? Could she have been referring to them and not the men in my life? I just didn't know. My head felt like it might implode with so many thoughts and feelings swarming around in it. I really needed a break.

"Hello?" Fujin waved a hand in front of my face, and I blinked. "Anyone in there?"

"Yeah," I stuttered and flushed. "Sorry, just a lot on my mind."

"I can imagine." Raijin nodded toward my stomach. "Firestar filled us in on the news. I suppose congratulations are in order?" His long hair falling over his face as he cocked his head to the side.

"I guess so," I answered, not quite sure how to respond. Or even how I felt about the matter. One baby was something I could handle but three? Trina thought we would be fine. I mean, it wasn't like I was doing this alone. I had three mates to help me.

Wait a second. Three men. Three babies. It couldn't be, could it?

I glanced at Trina my eyes wide. "You don't think there's one for …?" I danced my finger across the air in front of me.

"For each of your men?" Trina leveled a stare at me and shrugged. "Possibly. It's not unheard of. And really at this point, there's no telling what will happen. They could all be Firestar's, or one could be his and two one of the others. I can't tell from the equipment I have here."

"They could on Earth," Raijin offered up.

I looked at him in surprise. "You're right. They could. The machines they have there are crazy. They can see everything inside of you just by doing a scan. It's kind of like magic but … not." I tried my best to explain to Trina and then turned back to Raijin. "How'd you know?"

Raijin scratched the back of his head with a small smile. "Well, let's just say you're not the only one whose parents sent them away for a while."

Fujin chuckled and bumped his twin in the stomach with his elbow. "What Raijin's trying to be elusive about is that our father thought it best we know both worlds if we are going to rule. That way if—"

"If the worlds ever merged, we'd be prepared," Raijin finished, shooting a glare at his twin.

"That's actually a really good idea." Firestar stroked his jaw. I was happy to see his coloring had come back and that he wasn't on the verge of passing out. There could be only one dramatic person in this group, and that belonged to the pregnant lady, damn it!

"You want to take her to Earth?" Trina asked, her brow furrowed. "I'm not sure that's a good idea right now, not with everything going on."

Firestar shook his head. "No, not right now. After things calm down, maybe." He gave me a soft look. "It'd be nice to know more about our children before they are born."

I squeezed his hand and smiled. "Of course. We'll get a full checkout, and I'll even show you around some of my favorite places."

The thought of going back to Earth didn't cause the same feeling of relief as it used to. When this all started, I'd wanted nothing but to find a portal to take me back, but the longer I spent time with Jack and Raiden, the less I felt that way. Then Firestar joined the mix, and I couldn't imagine ever leaving without them. Any of them.

I pulled my shirt back over my belly and slid from the table. After a quick goodbye to Trina and a promise to take it easy, we headed back toward the meeting room. The twins followed behind us, not surprising since we were the only ones they knew around the North. They probably felt as out of place as the rest of us. Sans Jack of course.

"So, did they decide anything before you came to the infirmary?" I asked Firestar, leaning into him his arm wrapped around my shoulders.

"Not really." Firestar huffed. "They'd only started discussing other options when we realized we'd sent you off alone. The way it was going, I doubt they were able to agree on the time of the next meeting let alone a course of action."

A low growl trickled out of Firestar, tickling my side. I didn't blame him for being frustrated. We all were. We had little men and no resources at hand to help us. The only way we were going to get what we needed to save Raiden's kingdom was to ask for help from the other kingdoms. Though, I had a feeling the likelihood of either the South or the

West helping was as likely as Lady Nariko choosing to give up on her own.

"Can't you ask your father?" Raijin asked what I'd been thinking. "You are the heir to the West after all."

"As are you, Firestar." Fujin jumped in. "You both have armies just sitting in wait. Couldn't you send word explaining the matter and requesting their help?"

Firestar and I exchanged a look and then burst out laughing. The twins stared at us in confusion before I finally stopped long enough to take a breath.

"I don't know if you've ever met my father, but he's not exactly easy going like yours. I'd have to beg and plead, promise him my firstborn, and even then, he'd probably still say no." Okay, so I was exaggerating, but it wasn't that far off from the truth. My father only liked to get involved in another kingdom's affairs when it benefited him. Which usually meant he had something to hold over them. I couldn't think of a single thing the East had to offer the West.

"But you're mated to our brother. Shouldn't that obligate him to help?" Raijin tilted his head, his brow furrowed.

"The only obligation Lord Dannon has is to himself," Raiden explained, coming up to us as we approached Lord Fafnir's office. Jack followed close behind him, but the tribe leaders and Lord Fafnir were nowhere to be found.

"What about Lord Amun?" Raijin tried. "Won't he want to help his son?"

The guys and I exchanged a look, and then Firestar coughed, staring down at the floor and muttered something.

"What was that?" Fujin asked, taking a step closer. "I didn't quite make that out."

"My father doesn't know I'm not the only mate, okay?" Firestar growled and crossed his arms over his chest. "He thinks Maya and me are betrothed, and I'll be the next lord of the West, combining our kingdoms together."

"Well, that's awkward," Raijin smirked. "You have fun explaining that to him when you go ask for his help."

"Wait a second, I never said I'd do that." Firestar glowered. "Plus, the last time I was there, my men turned on me and tried to take Maya. I don't even know if we have any men to help out."

"Well, someone will have to give up their pride." Jack tucked his hands into his pockets, his chest no longer bare. I wanted to hit whoever found him a new shirt. There goes my eye candy.

"Why?" Firestar snapped, suspicion in his face. "Did you actually decide on something?"

Raiden and Jack exchanged a look, then Jack sighed. "It came down to the fact that we need more men before we can do anything. And since the unaligned are as likely to help us as Lady Nariko herself, that only leaves one of you two." He pointed a finger at Firestar and me. "So, who's it going to be?"

4

Sweat dripped down my face as I bit my lip. I focused on my hands, trying to envision the ball of fire I'd created many times before over the last few days. My eyes squinted hard and then sighed in defeat when I didn't even create a wisp of smoke.

"I give up." I collapsed on the ground of the training field, my breathing hard. "I think I've poofed my last fireball for today."

Firestar crossed his arms over his chest a few feet away from me, a stern expression on his face. "I don't think so. You've barely started your training, and if I'm going to be appealing to my father for help, then we have to get as much training in now as we can."

"But I need a break." I rubbed my stomach and stared at him meaningfully. "*We* need a break."

His gaze softened, and he offered me a hand, lifting me to my feet. I curled into his embrace and rested my head on his chest, the soothing beat of his heart calming my own. Since my little incident in Lord Fafnir's office, we'd been training to make sure I didn't accidentally set anyone else on fire. Though Firestar had been a bit more enthusiastic about the training than the others because of the decision to go visit his father.

Though Firestar had agreed to ask his father for men, I was still going to send word to my own father. That way, our chances of getting help were higher. The guys had a bet going on about who would agree to help. Firestar didn't have much faith in either of our fathers.

"I don't want to leave you," Firestar said after a moment. His hand stroked my hair, and he pressed his lips to my forehead. "The new powers aside, you now have three babies to take care of." Firestar scowled. "And it's not like you have a lot of allies here. We never did find Jack's ex-bitch."

I patted his chest and chuckled at his growl. "It'll be fine. I have Raiden and Jack. Plus, the twins are here. Besides, I think Lord Fafnir feels a bit bad about Gretchen attacking me on his watch. I don't think he will be letting anything else happen to me."

"He better not," Firestar grumbled.

Sighing, I pushed away from him. "You should be more worried about any more powers appearing." I glanced down at my baby bump. "One baby with powers from within the womb is more than enough."

Approaching footsteps drew my attention to Jack and Raiden. They'd be dealing with the other tribe leaders while Firestar helped me train. I released Firestar and hugged Raiden, who got to me first. His fingers threaded into my hair, tilting my head to the side as he took my mouth in a passionate kiss. His tongue stroked mine, making a pleasant tingle settle between my thighs. His growl rumbled against me, and he held me tighter, probably having scented my arousal.

Jack cleared his throat next to us, forcing Raiden to release me with a cheeky grin. He slapped me on the ass before letting me go to Jack. Breathing hard and face flushed, I shyly placed my hand on Jack's chest.

"How do I compete with that?" he asked, sarcasm dripping from his words, but I could hear the insecurity in his voice.

Standing on my tip toes, I wrapped my arms around his neck. "There's no competition," I murmured before pressing my lips to his. Our kiss was languid where Raiden's had been fast and intense. Both different but both giving me a burning need to have them naked and inside of me.

"Happy?" I asked when we drew back.

Jack caressed the side of my face with a small smile. "Always." He then glanced at my stomach and pressed a hand to the swell of it. "How are our children? Any signs of whose they are?"

To say the guys had been surprised about the announcement of a trio over a single would be an understatement. Actually, Jack had barely twitched. His only reaction had been a slight widening of his eyes, unlike Raiden, who'd been so overjoyed I'd had to get the twins to pry him off me. Now, they were determined to find out if the other two babies were theirs. Though I'd told them on more than one occasion that it didn't really matter.

Must be a guy thing.

"They," I started with a distraught look, "are tired and famished. And no, no signs of more powers, thankfully." The disappointed look on Raiden and Jack's faces were comical. "Oh, stop it. I understand your eagerness to find out, but I wouldn't be upset if none of them showed any more gifts. The heartburn is bad enough." I placed a hand on my chest and winced.

The hand on my palm started to cool and then, before I knew it, became freezing. Jack was the first to react. He reached out and grabbed my hand, pulling it away from my chest before I could freeze myself solid. His touch, unlike Firestar's who had only amplified my powers, seemed to calm them.

"Well, that answers that." Firestar snorted and then smirked at Raiden. "Guess there's only one odd man out now."

Raiden glowered and pouted at the same time. A weird but adorable combination. I smacked Firestar on the arm and frowned. "Don't poke fun. It's not nice or fair to anyone."

"Oh, so he can make fun of me all the time, but I can't?" Firestar argued, his fists on his hips.

"That's different," Raiden grumbled, still pouting. "I'm not teasing you about your virility."

"Just that I have a small dick," Firestar snapped, causing Raiden to grin.

Shrugging, Raiden said, "What can I say? You're an easy target."

"In any case," Jack interrupted with a frown, "you shouldn't push so hard. While training is important, we don't want you to end up hurting yourself or the baby with too much training."

"But now that she has your power as well, isn't that all the more reason to train?" Firestar stood up straighter, as if he could use his size to intimidate Jack into agreeing with him. The poor guy, when was he going to learn?

Jack arched an elegant brow. "And when she goes into premature labor from the stress, will you be the one telling Trina?"

Firestar blanched at Jack's question. I giggled at his reaction. A big guy like Firestar afraid of my tiny medic? Now, that was something.

"I suppose you're right," Firestar finally conceded. "We have time to train and rest." He turned and lifted me up into his arms until I was cradled like a baby.

"Where are you going?" I laughed, wrapping my arms around his neck. The others just looked on with growing amusement. Traitors.

"You need rest," Firestar smirked.

"I can still walk." I rolled my eyes but smiled broadly.

"But" - Firestar lowered his lips to just by my ear - "the more energy you spend on that, the less you have for more enjoyable activities."

Swallowing at his implications, a hot burning need slid through me, and my arms tightened around him. "Now?"

Firestar wagged his eyebrows up and down and then called out to the guys trailing behind us. "I'm going to get Maya tucked into bed for a nap. Don't wait up for us."

"Sure, you are," Raiden called after us. "Make sure you take care of your dick. You know, it being small and all."

A growl came from Firestar's chest, vibrating through me, but he didn't respond. I could hear Jack reprimanding Raiden as we made our way back into the house. I was kind of surprised how well the guys got along in general. If I had been on Earth, they would have beaten each other to death from jealousy or plain annoyance.

Mostly in Raiden's case. He sometimes didn't know when enough was enough. That'd get him ran over by a car just because.

I'm sorry officer, he just wouldn't stop talking. I chuckled at the mental image.

Even some dragons would have a challenging time living the way we did. We weren't monoga-mous by any means, but most didn't co-exist the way we did. One of my tutors had five mates, and they rotated who she spent time with based on a schedule. The men rarely saw each other except on special occasions, and those were scarce as well.

I couldn't handle that. I needed to see them all, every day. I couldn't imagine not being allowed to see the others because it wasn't their day. It made me happy that they got along so well.

I thought back to Raiden and Firestar's little argument. Good thing Jack was never far away. I had a feeling he'd be playing referee a lot in the days to come. With the upcoming fight, I worried if we would even live long enough for it to be a problem.

My dark thoughts were interrupted by Firestar kicking the bedroom door open. He'd brought me to his bedroom. The dark browns of the fur cover on his bed tempted me to strip my clothes off and rub my skin all over their softness.

"Thought we'd be less likely to be disturbed in my room." Firestar gave a wolfish grin before stalking across the room and dropping me on the bed.

I bounced slightly but didn't complain, my eyes trained on Firestar as he ripped his shirt over his head. His thick muscles flexed under my perusal. I licked my lips and met his hot gaze, his canines flashed, and his hands dropped to his waist. My breath held, waiting for him to undo the ties of his pants. I had seen the guys without clothes plenty of times before, but it never got old. I always felt like a cat in heat, eager and willing to get my mouth on every inch of lickable skin as I could. Now was no different.

My legs parted on their own as Firestar released himself from his pants, the long length of him hard and throbbing as if aching for my touch. Firestar grunted at my movement and rumbled, "Eager, are we?"

"Always," I breathed, wrapping my hand around him. His breath hitched as he let me stroke him for a few moments. Before I could get too into it though, he pushed my hand away and crawled onto the bed.

"Not today." Firestar prowled toward me, causing me to lie back on the bed. "Today, I want to be inside of you when I go. I might be gone a while. I need to engrain the feel of you on my dick."

I threw my head back and laughed. "And you haven't done that by now?"

Firestar's lips traced mine lightly. "Of course, but it sounded so much more romantic than what I had in mind."

"And what would that be?" His hand found its way beneath my shirt and pinched my nipple, making me gasp. "Are you going to fuck me into your memory?"

Firestar smirked. "Something like that." His fingers twisted and pulled at my aching tips. My back arched in response and a small keening noise fell from my lips. "I can't have Raiden getting it into your head that I'm anything smaller than I am."

In between gasps, I giggled. "That's not possible."

He pressed his length to my clothed heat and ground against me. "Does this feel small to you?" I bucked my hips against him, the need to have him closer becoming overwhelming. "Well, does it?"

Raiden would have been proud. I'd thought he was the master of teasing, but Firestar was giving him a run for his money. Though I'd never say such a thing. Raiden's little jokes about Firestar were obviously getting to him. I couldn't let him think he's any less than the others. Even though we all knew that Jack was the big boy of the bunch.

"No," I moaned and rolled my hips against him, wrapping my legs around his waist to pull him closer. "Not small at all."

"That's what I thought." Firestar shifted me to

the side and, with one fell swoop, rid me of my pants and underwear. The cool air of the room hit my slickened heat, and my eyes rolled back in my head. I didn't even notice when Firestar ripped my shirt off my body. I'd get on to him later, I told myself.

A hot wet mouth replaced Firestar's hand on my breast, his tongue circling around the peak, tugging on it until I cried out. His other hand played along the inside of my thighs, stroking back and forth until he came just inches away from where I wanted him to be and then back again.

"Firestar!" I let out a growl of frustration. "Enough of the teasing."

He released my breast with a loud pop, his mouth trailing down my stomach and hovering over my dripping core. He blew on it, and my hand grabbed at the back of his head. He shook me off, not letting me take control. "Now, now. Patience. I want to make memories, not some quick fuck in between meetings."

"That was one time," I snarled. "And months ago. My patience is not what it used to be."

"Was it ever?" Firestar chuckled between my thighs, making me groan in ecstasy. I opened my mouth to argue but pulled in a hard breath as his tongue lapped at me. My fingers tightened on him, and I rotated my hips into his mouth, begging for more.

Thick fingers found their way into my entrance without warning. My hips jumped off the bed as they thrust into me, his mouth pulling hard on my bundle of nerves. It didn't take long for me to find my release, and Firestar wasted no time in replacing his fingers with his length. We groaned in unison as he pushed into me. Every one of my guys knew exactly how to play my body, but nothing beat having them inside of me, moving together as one.

With each stroke, I felt him deep within me, bringing me higher and higher. He leaned down so that our chests pressed together as much as they could with my stomach. I savored this position as long as I could, the face to face contact. I knew our three babies eventually would grow so large it would seem like a small planet separated us, and it would be harder to handle this position. Though there were many others we could try that Firestar and the others were just as proficient in.

My nails dug into Firestar's back as I screamed my second release, my toes curling and my nerves tingling all over. Firestar thrust a few more times into me before he tensed and let out a heavy breath, signaling his own orgasm. I didn't immediately push him off nor did he seem in a hurry to move.

Propping himself up on his elbows, he stared down at me with such adoration that my eyes prickled with tears. I didn't know how I deserved such a wonderful mate. All of them. They had their faults, but they were mine. No one could ever make me feel the way they did, nor would I want them to try.

"Promise me something." Firestar stroked the side of my face with his thumb. "While I'm gone, you will take it easy. None of this 'I'm a grown ass woman and can't take care of myself' crap."

I snorted. "This coming from the man who just tried to make me train longer."

"Hey!" Firestar pointed a finger at my face. "That was for your own good as well. If you can control your fire magic, then I will feel better about leaving you behind. And now that you have Jack's power as well ..." he trailed off, but I knew what he meant.

"More powers are a good thing," I explained to him. "I've been bitching about the lack of benefits on my end." Firestar raised a brow in amusement. "Why should you guys get all the cool abilities and I get what?" I gestured down to my stomach. "Fat. That's what I get."

"And beautiful," Firestar added, leaning down to kiss my stomach. I smiled despite myself and shoved at his shoulder. Firestar's smile went serious once more. "I mean it, Maya. While Jack and Raiden are here too, I don't want you to leave either of their sides. Even the twins would be fine, but we don't know who might be in Lord Fafnir's camp that might want to hurt you or our children." His hand slid across my stomach as he said it.

I placed mine on top of his and met his worried gaze. "I promise."

5

"**S**houldn't you take someone with you?" I argued for what felt like the millionth time. "What if someone attacks you? I'm not the only one with enemies out there."

Firestar adjusted his bag onto his back and gave me a look. "I'll be faster on my own. We need all our people here with you."

"No, we don't," I countered, grabbing his arm so he couldn't dismiss me. "I will be fine. At least take the twins."

"They're needed here." Firestar shook his head. "If something happens and they need to head to the front, how are they going to do that if they are with me on the other side of Waesigar?"

I shrugged. "Fly?"

Chuckling, Firestar kissed my forehead. "I'll be fine. I'll stick to the high altitudes so I won't be seen and rest in hidden areas. Don't worry about me. You just work on controlling those powers of yours."

"Not worry?" I scoffed, hugging him tightly. "That's impossible, but I will work on my new powers." I grinned up at him. "Just wait, I'll be as good as you by the time you get back."

Firestar snorted. "No one is as good as me, but if anyone could be, it'd be you."

"Are you prepared?" Jack asked, coming up next to us.

He and Raiden had done their best to give us as much alone time as possible before Firestar left. I appreciated it, but I also missed them. I hadn't been lying about not being able to handle getting to be with only one of them. They had all dug their claws into my heart, and it would be hard for me to pry any of them out.

"As prepared as I'm going to get." Firestar shifted his bag again and then offered Jack a hand. "You'll take care of her, won't you?"

"Need you ask?" Jack cocked his head to the side and took Firestar's hand in his. They shook, and then Jack stepped away, allowing Raiden to step forward. Firestar tried to offer him his hand as well, but of course, being who he was, Raiden bypassed it and pulled Firestar into a hug.

I held back a giggle as Firestar awkwardly patted Raiden on the back and then shoved him away when he whispered something I couldn't hear. Firestar had a scowl on his face as Raiden laughed and dodged his swing.

"Will you ever grow up?" Firestar asked with an exasperated huff.

"Not likely," Raiden smirked and then wrapped an arm around my shoulders. "But don't worry, I won't let it interfere with my duties. I promise not a single strand of hair will come to harm on our precious mate's head." I raised a brow at him and then he quickly added, "That was not begged for, that is."

Firestar groaned and rubbed a hand over his face. "Maybe I shouldn't go. I could just send my father a message like you did yours." Firestar gestured to me with a hand, his unease to leave really showing on his face, completely the opposite of what his expression had been moments before.

Pushing out of Raiden's grasp, I took hold of Firestar's hands. "You will be fine. I will be fine. And you can't send a message because you know your father will never believe that you would ask for help.

Especially since he doesn't know the whole story. He will be more likely to offer up help if you go to him in person. My father will understand my lack of wanting to travel." I placed a hand on my stomach with a soft look. "Besides, I messaged my sister, not my father. She'll be more diplomatic about it than I ever could."

"Good idea." Firestar nodded and then took one last look at our little group. "You know, I never did find that dagger for you, like I promised. Maybe you could work on that while I'm gone? Keep you out of trouble."

Jack gave a short laugh. "You know that's not how it works. Trouble finds her."

"Isn't that the truth?" Raiden scoffed. "We could be cooped up in our rooms the entire time you are gone, and she'd still find some way to end up in the infirmary. Actually," - Raiden slid his arm around my waist - "that's not a bad idea. Want to fuck like rabbits for a few weeks? We could have your food delivered."

I rolled my eyes and didn't even bother to answer. Instead, I said to Firestar, "Be careful. I'll be thinking of you every day." I moved into Firestar's arms and pressed my mouth to his in a short but passionate kiss. When it ended, I had a bad feeling in my stomach. The kind that usually meant some-thing would happen soon. Shoving the feeling down, I forced a smile on my face and hoped he didn't notice.

"Alright," Firestar sighed and pulled away from me. "I guess I can't wait any longer. I'll send word once I have arrived. And you let me know if you hear from your father first." He pointed a finger at me, and I nodded. He turned away from us, his fiery wings appearing on his back. With one last wave, he lifted off into the sky and then he was gone.

Wrapping my arms around myself, I frowned. I didn't like this. I knew it was important and it had to happen, but it didn't make it any better. I hoped the feeling I had was just anxiety in general and not some premonition. If one of our children had Jack's abilities, it was all too easy for them to have some kind of seer power as well. That was one ability I did not want to have.

"Come on." Raiden ushered me back into the house. "Dinner will be served soon. You don't want to miss out." He leaned in close and whispered conspiratorially. "Carl told me he just got a new batch of raspberries."

My lip twitched up in a grimace. During the

first trimester, I had longed for nothing but the yummy warm goodness of the palace cook's famous raspberry tarts, the very thought of them now made my stomach curl. "No more raspberries please."

"What?" Raiden gasped his hand going to his chest and then looked at Jack who followed quietly beside us. "Do you hear this nonsense? Maya, the queen of the raspberries, is refusing such a mouth-watering treat?"

"Since the babies would rather drink their own embryonic fluid than eat another raspberry tart ..." I half gagged just trying to get the words out. In total opposition, my stomach growled, demanding it be fed. "Please tell me there will be something else at this meal? Maybe something with pickles and maple syrup?"

Raiden made a disgusted face but had the restraint not to say anything about it for once. Jack placed his hand on my lower back and guided me into the dining hall without another word.

Carl popped out with a tray just as we sat down, but Raiden quickly intercepted him with a shake of his head. He spoke rapidly in hushed tones to Carl who went from delighted to horrified. Then Carl turned his eyes to me, and I think I just lost a friend.

"What did you say to him?" I hissed when

Raiden sat beside me, keeping my eyes on Carl who kept giving me the evil eye.

Raiden shrugged. "I told him you didn't like the tarts anymore."

"No, you didn't," I accused, daring him to lie to me. "If you'd said that he wouldn't have looked at me like I'd just killed his puppy."

"Well," - Raiden moved his head from side to side - "I might not have said it so nicely."

I threw my napkin at him. "God, Raiden. You don't piss off the cook. Everyone knows that!"

Jack shook his head, disappointed in Raiden as much as I was. Okay, maybe my expression was more enraged than disappointed, but that also might be the hormones and the hunger talking. Either way, I would have felt better about my outrage if Jack had displayed a little bit more emotion as well.

"I'm sorry," Raiden patted my hand. "I didn't mean to upset you. I really wanted to get you your pickles and syrup."

I was only half listening to his apology as Carl approached our table with a plate. He sat it down in front of me with as much indignation as possible. Before he could scurry away back to the kitchen, I grabbed the sleeve of his shirt.

"Carl," I started, putting my best puppy dog face on. "I think there's been some misunderstanding. Whatever Raiden said, forget it." I waved a hand in front of me. Carl gave me an incredulous frown, not at all believing me. I'd have up to up the ante. "Look, Carl, you know I'm pregnant. Well, sometimes the little guys don't always cooperate." Carl seemed to calm a bit, so I quickly added, "I would love to be able to eat some of your delicious raspberry tarts but the triplets."

Carl's eyes widened at the bombshell I'd just dropped. Seemed to be a pattern around here. "You're having triplets?" he asked, leaning against the edge of the table. "I didn't know."

"Yeah," I sighed and shook my head. "Neither did we until the other day. And you understand how that makes me outnumbered in the what goes in my stomach department, right?"

"Of course, of course," Carl replied, nodding enthusiastically. "And don't worry about the tarts. They'll be there when your stomach settles." He nodded toward my lower half. "If you have any new cravings, please don't hesitate to let me know."

"Thank you so much, Carl." I cooed, fluttering my lashes after him. When he was gone, I turned back to my plate and the guys staring me down. "What?" I lifted a shoulder.

"You just flirted with him." Raiden grinned cheekily, exchanging a look with Jack, who looked way too amused for the serious one of the bunch.

"I did not." My voice rose as I picked my fork up and stabbed one of the syrup coated pickles.

"Maya." The way Jack said my name was the way he said it in the bedroom, which in itself should have told me he wanted something.

"I didn't!" I insisted once more.

"You fluttered your eyelashes at him," Raiden pointed out with smug satisfaction.

"And your voice lowered in pitch." Jack's lips curled up at the edges.

I took a large bite of my pickle to give myself some time, grimacing as I forced it down. What they hell had I been thinking? Pickles and maple syrup? Disgusting.

Setting my fork down, I shifted in my seat. "So, what?" They just stared at me. "Fine. So maybe I put on the charm a bit. But you," - I pointed a finger at Raiden - "just about put me on the shit list for the only man in this area who can give me some satisfaction."

"Oh," Raiden grasped his chest like he'd been shot. "That's cold, Maya."

"Raiden," Jack said slowly with a sly move of his head, "I think we may need to work together to rectify this obvious misunderstanding."

"I think you're right." Raiden grinned like a Cheshire cat. "Clearly, we aren't doing our job, if the cook is getting special treatment."

My mouth went dry at the salacious leers. I shifted uncomfortably in my seat, my panties completely ruined from the visual I had of the two of them tag teaming me. If I'd known they'd react this way to a little jealousy, I might have thought about doing it on purpose.

"So," - Raiden stood up and offered me a hand - "what are we waiting for?"

I reached out to take his hand when my stomach rumbled once more. Damn my stomach and its constant need for food. I sank back into my seat and sighed.

"Sorry, guys. As much as I'd love to spend the rest of the evening finding out how absolutely incredible you two would be as a pre-meditated team, I'm afraid we've been outvoted." I pointed both hands at my stomach. "Food comes first."

"Of course," Jack agreed, nodding toward my

plate. "We'll wait. You'll need your energy after all." The way he said it made a delightful shiver run through me, and I was just a second away from saying fuck it, but then I remembered the plate in front of me.

Glaring down at the combination of sour and sweet, I forced the bile back. "I think I'm going to need Carl again." When Raiden and Jack made a sound of displeasure, I quickly added, "Just for food. I swear. I can't eat this crap. I'm disowning whatever one of our children wanted this disgusting mess." I shoved the plate as far away from me as possible.

Raiden chuckled and waved Carl over again. "I think we can take care of our girl."

I sagged in my chair. Thank God. Because I sure as hell couldn't.

After dinner, we had to put a pin in our threesome. An unfortunate belch that turned into me knocking the power out in the entire house kind of put a damper on the mood and a bullseye on my dysfunctional pregnancy.

"For the last time," I argued, stomping my foot slightly. "How was I supposed to know that I had to keep an eye on my bodily functions now? It's not like there's a manual for a magical pregnancy. Though that'd be helpful," I muttered the last bit to myself. For once, I wished I was on Earth where folks chronicled their own bowel movements. There I could at least Google what was going on with me. You know, if dragons existed there.

I shook my weird thoughts away and glanced back to the guys, who were staring at me like they didn't believe me. Typical.

Jack lit a candle and handed it to Raiden before turning to me, another burning in his other hand. "The important thing is that no one got hurt." He gave me a look that made me think there was a but coming on. "However …" I knew it! Jack continued after he paused for effect, "We really need to work on your new abilities before that changes. My uncle is not amused by your little hiccup."

"I burped," I corrected him. "I didn't hiccup. It was a burp. And God forbid, I do anything to upset our host." Jack gave me a look that had me adding, "Who has been nothing but kind to use and is even helping us take back Raiden's kingdom. Really, he's a standup guy. We shouldn't do anything to get ourselves thrown out."

"Exactly," Jack concurred, clearly not amused by my theatrics. "Since Firestar is away, we need to work on your training. Obviously, I'll work with you on my abilities and—"

"I'll do mine!" Raiden practically bounced with joy, having been the only odd man out on this crazy train. I'd have hit him for being so excited about a new power when I clearly didn't need or want one, but the thought that one of my babies belonged to each of them made me happy. No one was left out. No hard feelings. Plus, that meant when they were born, I could shove one at each of them and take a nap. It was a win-win.

"Sounds great, guys," I smiled, but it wasn't very enthusiastic as I stifled a yawn. "But can we work on that tomorrow? I'm pooped and could do with a bit of rest." A weird pull on my stomach, like bubbles popping, made me frown. "Maybe a lot of sleep."

"Of course." Jack held his arm out and led me out of his bedroom and into my own. I half noticed Raiden didn't follow after us but was too tired to wonder too much about it. I placed my candle on my nightstand and sat on the edge of the bed. Jack knelt before me and, before I could ask what he was doing, had my shoes off my feet.

He moved to my dresser and brought my nightgown over to me. I started to take my shirt off, but Jack stopped me. Dropping hands, I let him unlace the neck of my shirt and slide over my head. His hands dipped down to my waist, and a small tingle of arousal spread down below. Jack offered me a small knowing smile but didn't try to act on his knowledge. Urging me to lift my hips, he drew my pants down my legs, leaving me in nothing but my underwear.

His appreciative gaze scanned over my form before settling over my stomach. Instead of helping me into my nightgown, he leaned in close and pressed the side of his face to my stomach. I jumped slightly at the cool contact of his skin but didn't push him away.

"It's remarkable." His voice rumbled against my skin. "I never thought I would be the kind of man who would care so much about being a father. But here I am." He glanced up at me, an expression on his face I couldn't describe. "A gorgeous mate and not one but three children on the way. It was truly a blessing the day my uncle asked me to go to the West."

My face flushed at his intense gaze. "I don't know about that. No one's ever said anything about me was a blessing. More like a curse but maybe that's just my winning personality." I shot him a cheeky grin.

Jack chuckled. "See, only you can make me laugh in such a serious situation. I love you, Maya." He cupped my shoulders and drew me close. "I couldn't stand it if anything happened to you or our children."

"I love you too," I muttered into his neck. This whole conversation was getting me worked up and not in a good way. I'd had enough of my raging emotions and didn't need any more touching moments to make me bawl like a baby. I was sure I'd have enough of those in the coming months.

"Now." Jack pulled back and picked up the discarded nightgown. He slipped it over my head and then brushed his lips across mine. "Get some sleep. We will start training again in the morning. Who knows? Maybe by the time Firestar gets back, you'll be able to knock him on his ass."

I laughed at the visual as Jack moved away. I grabbed his hand before he could leave and dragged him back down to me. Pressing my lips to his in a hungry, desperate sort of way, I tangled my hands in his hair, keeping him there. When we withdrew to breathe, Jack let out another chuckle this time husky and low.

"You make it hard for a man to leave you, my love." Jack's pale eyes, so full of lust and need, made my skin flush with desire.

"Then don't."

Jack paused for a moment and then shook his head. "As much as I'd love to crawl into this bed with you and make sweet love to your luscious body,

I have to talk with Raiden about your training, and you need your rest."

My bottom lip stuck out as my last attempt to get him to give in, but he simply thumbed it slightly with a sigh. "Do not look so distraught. There will be plenty of time for other activities when you aren't a walking time bomb."

"I am not!" My pouting face now turned to irritation. Jack raised a brow at me, and I slumped on the bed. "I just don't know how to control my powers yet or my emotions or my body functions." I threw my hands up in the air with an over exaggerated sigh. "Fine, you win. I'll go to sleep." I moved under the covers and then pointed a finger at him. "But don't think that means I won't have naughty dreams of my promised threesome that never happened."

"You wound me." Jack placed a hand on his chest, mocking Raiden's earlier movements.

"Yeah, yeah," I rolled my eyes.

"Good night, Maya." Jack pressed his lips to my cheek and caressed the side of my face.

"Good night." I snuggled down in the bed, my eyes trained on Jack until he left the room, the door shut tight behind him. I turned over and stared at the lit candle, watching the flame dance this way and that. Before I knew it, I was asleep.

For the first time in a while, I didn't have pleasant dreams. My mind filled with terrors that I could only assume my waking mind couldn't deal with. Not that I could blame it; the last few weeks had more than enough trauma for everyone.

Standing in the dining hall of Lord Fafnir's house, I found myself as the one Jack was yelling at. My eyes wide, I searched out where I should have been standing and saw Gretchen in my place. The smug grin on her lips turned my pity for her to rage as she wrapped her arms around my men.

"You are dead to me." Jack's word resonated with me, shaking me to the very core. Panic filled me, and my hand instantly went to my stomach where it had already swelled to that of nine months.

"You'd leave me now? When I need you most?" But, as with Gretchen, my words weren't acknowledged. My body trembled as I watched Jack walk away from me and over to where Gretchen stood. She pulled Jack into her embrace, her face that of gleeful victory and suddenly all I wanted was to kill.

A heavy weight filled my hand, and I glanced down to see the lost dagger in it. Tightening my grip on the hilt, I stalked toward the grinning foursome, my intent all too clear in my movements. I aimed the blade for Gretchen, my every desire to slice open her chest and find out if she really did have a heart, but the dagger found a home in someone else.

Jack jumped in the way of my attack and now lay bleeding on the ground, his eyes wide open in death. My hands came up to my mouth as I stared down at what I'd done. The dagger fell from my hands and clattered on the ground as more hands grabbed me, pulling me away from Jack's corpse.

"I didn't mean it," I cried as they dragged me away, kicking and screaming. "I didn't mean it!"

Forced out of the dining room, my hands were bound, and a dirty piece of cloth was tied around my mouth, making me gag. I tried to yell around the cloth, but it was no use. My captors had no sympathies for me. As if it couldn't get any worse, a bag went over my head, and everything was black.

Shoved into a confined space, I bumped around in some kind of vehicle. Possibly a carriage. I could hear muffled talking around me but couldn't see anything through the hood on my head. The hood made my heavy breathing heat up the interior, making the already musky hood smell even worse.

If I didn't get out of here soon, I knew I was going to vomit. In fact, it was happening right now.

Jerking up in bed, I barely leaned over the bed in time before my stomach emptied itself into the bucket I'd put by the bed. Sweaty and hot, I wiped the back of my hand over my mouth and groaned. Talk about some dream. The babies affected me enough during the waking hours; couldn't they at least leave my dreams alone?

Apparently not.

I eased off the other side of the bed, the light streaming through the windows and making my eyes squint. Practically blind, I somehow made my way to the bathroom where I rinsed my mouth and brushed my teeth like they would fall out at any moment.

As I grabbed the bucket next to the bed, I thought about that dream. It had been disturbingly vivid. I still remembered what it felt like to have the bag over my head. The taste of the cloth still clung to my tongue, no matter how much I scrubbed it. I'd heard pregnancy makes your dreams more real, but this was ridiculous.

Finished with making myself presentable, I headed for the door. Just as I opened it, I found myself face-to-face with Jack. Surprise filled his eyes before he settled into a blank expression.

"Hey," I said softly, tucking a hair behind my ear. "What's up?"

Jack inclined his head slightly. "Nothing of importance. Are you ready to head to breakfast? You should eat something before we train. Wouldn't want you to burn out too quickly, like yesterday."

Shutting the door behind me, I walked alongside Jack as we headed to breakfast. "Have we heard anything from Firestar yet?"

"He hasn't been gone that long," Jack reminded me with soft eyes. "I understand you miss him, but you have to trust he will be fine."

"I guess," I muttered, still not convinced. Last night's dream was still fresh in my mind making it hard to believe anything will be alright.

We met Raiden in front of the dining hall, and he embraced me quickly before cupping my face in his hands. "You don't look like you slept a wink."

Giving him a weak smile, I sighed. "Is it that obvious?"

"Just a bit." Raiden held his pointer and thumb finger an inch from each other.

Rubbing a hand over my face, I sighed even

more heavily. "My dreams are getting worse. This time, I literally felt like I was in my nightmare."

Raiden hugged me close and kissed the top of my head. "Maybe you shouldn't sleep alone from now on? Might help your dreams."

"Maybe," I agreed as we sat at the breakfast table. When Carl brought out our meals, he waited at my side. I glanced up at him and then realized he wanted to be sure I wasn't going to send my food back. Turning back to my plate, I scooped up a substantial portion of eggs and put it in my mouth. "Mmmm." I nodded, smiling at him. It seemed to satisfy him enough that he headed back to the kitchen.

We ate our meal in silence for a few moments before I broke it. "So, what's on today's agenda?"

"Well, Raiden and I are going to start helping you go through some breathing exercises," Jack answered, picking his cup up.

"What for?" My brow furrowed.

"To help you control your emotions." Raiden piled eggs and meat onto his plate before showering it with syrup. The sight of it made my stomach churn.

Reaching for the teacup Carl had been kind enough to provide for me, I took a long drink of it before saying, "I don't think breathing exercises are the answer."

Jack sat his utensils down and stared at me hard. "Why?"

I stared right back with an edge of defiance. "Because I have a problem."

"Yes, you do." Raiden pointed his fork at me, a piece of syrup-covered meat on the end. I forced back the urge to throw up and turned to Jack.

"Can't we just go look for the dagger, like Firestar suggested? I can practice my breathing and magic without being anywhere near civilians."

"Why would you want to do that?" Jack demanded, an icy bite in his tone. "It's gone. You should let what's dead stay buried."

"Well, I can't do that, and I won't," I snapped before he could argue with me further.

Jack seemed about ready to explode, but when Raiden cleared his throat, giving him a meaningful look that I didn't understand, he sighed. His face smoothed over and a soft, almost pitying look took over.

"You are too nice for your own good, Maya." Jack took my hand in his, rubbing his thumb over the back of it. "If it makes you feel better, I guess I can't argue."

"I guess not," I couldn't help but quip back, earning me a rightly earned glare.

Before Jack could chastise me further, Lord Fafnir approached with three other men at his side. We stopped eating and turned to the group, nodding our heads in greeting.

"I thought I might find you three here." Lord Fafnir glanced around the table with a curious look. "I'm sorry to interrupt your meal, but a rather large army is demanding entrance into my town." Jack and Raiden jumped to their feet at his words, but the lord didn't seem worried but looked to me. "And the one leading them is someone I can only assume is your sister."

"Aeis?" I got to my own feet.

"Well, you did send word for her to send an army," Raiden reminded me, following me out of the dining room.

I scowled at him. "Yeah, but I didn't expect her to come with it!"

7

We followed Lord Fafnir down toward the entrance hall. There we found a group of guards and leading them, my sister, Aeis.

Aeis should have been the heir to the throne of Western Waesigar, which she was until a few months ago, when she found out she couldn't have children. That was when my father suddenly pulled me out of my life on Earth and demanded I pick a mate and get pregnant.

Aeis had always been the perfect child and the perfect warrior, with long legs and a curvy build. She had the right attitude for ruling as well. A no-nonsense, mother-knows-best kind of personality that I had always hated growing up. Something I would have killed for now. Especially since it could have been my father showing up instead of her.

"Maya!" Aeis cried out when she saw me, her arms out wide as she pulled me into her embrace. Her leather armor pressed against the side of my face, the fur lining her coat tickling my nose.

"Hey, Aeis." I held my sister tightly, inhaling the scent of home lingering on her person. I leaned back and tugged on the braid of her dark hair with a grin. "It's good to see you."

Her emerald eyes looked me over as she held me by the shoulders. "And I you, but when did you get so fat?"

Okay, I take it back. My father would have been just fine.

I shook my head and smiled. "I'm pregnant, that tends to happen."

Her mouth dropped open. "I thought you were still faking. I didn't know you were actually pregnant."

"Well," I shrugged, "I am. Sorry, I didn't send word, we've been pretty busy."

Aeis glanced around the entrance hall of Lord Fafnir's house and nodded. "I can see that." She then turned her attention to the two men close behind me. "And I see you haven't scared these two off yet but" - she leaned to the side, her eyes searching - "I don't see the hothead anywhere."

Raiden chuckled and nudged Jack behind me. "Hothead."

"Firestar," I corrected her, sending Raiden a look over my shoulder, "went to ask his father for his help. Obviously," - I gestured down to my stomach - "you can see why I couldn't do the same."

"Lady Aeis, we are so happy to have you as a guest here," Lord Fafnir interrupted our little chat from where he stood off to the side. There was a slight glint in his eyes, showing his amusement at watching our back-and-forth. What could I say? My family and I had a weird relationship.

"Thank you, Lord Fafnir. But please, just Aeis." She smiled her diplomatic smile. "I hope we haven't caused you any alarm. It's hard to hide such a large army."

While Lord Fafnir and my sister had a good chuckle, I cocked my head to the side. "How many men did you bring? And why are you here anyway? I only asked for the army, not you."

Aeis's laughter died off, and she sniffed. "Well, excuse me for wanting to see my sister. And I brought every soldier except those already on missions and what was necessary to keep our kingdom secure."

"You know that's not what I meant," I tried to apologize and then added, "You brought the whole army?" I gaped at her and then shook my head. "Not that I'm complaining just … that's a lot of people. Where did you stick them all?"

"They're over the next ridge in an open field, making camp." Aeis gestured outside. "We didn't want to assume Lord Fafnir would have enough room for everyone. And no offense …" She glanced around the house. "But you're a bit humbler in your needs."

Lord Fafnir didn't get upset, but he did lace his hands in front of him a sign that he didn't appreciate her comments. I didn't see how he could be offended by it though. It wasn't like she said it was a crap heap, which it wasn't. I liked the smaller palace compared to my father's and the rest of the lords. It was homey. You didn't get lost after five minutes.

I could see how Lord Fafnir might not see it that way though. My father and Lord Dannon were the types of pointing those kinds of things out, often and incessantly.

"Either way," Aeis quickly continued when Lord Fafnir didn't respond how she expected, "I am grateful for your hospitality while I help my sister and her men."

Nodding, Lord Fafnir glanced off to the side to a lingering servant. "I'll have a room readied for you. Please, let us know if there is anything else I can do to make your stay more … humble." With that, Lord Fafnir inclined his head to Jack and headed down the hall, leaving us alone with my sister.

"Man, you still know how to clear a room." I shook my head and laughed. "I don't know why I always thought you were the diplomatic one of us. You were also the less tactful if that's believable."

Aeis shrugged. "What can I say? Sometimes my mouth gets away from me." She unbuttoned her jacket and draped it over her arm, for once she wasn't wearing a ridiculously impractical dress she insisted on wearing in court. Her shirt clung to her chest, the neckline dipping down to show a hint of cleavage. The pants seemed poured onto her legs, her boots stopping just beneath her knee. I'd never seen my sister look so fierce and hot at the same time.

"Did you take that from my closet?" I asked, pulling at her shirt sleeve.

"No," Aeis scoffed, and I gave her a disbelieving

look. "Is it that hard to believe I own something battle-ready? I was the first in my class after all."

"I think you look lovely." Jack supplied, and I rolled my eyes.

"I didn't say she didn't look good, just that it looked like mine. Of course, she looks good. She's my sister for God's sake." Looping my arm through hers, I guided her away from the doors and toward further into the house. Her guards followed us. I didn't bother trying to tell them to take off, I knew they wouldn't. My father might have me as the heir, but she was still his favorite. He'd have strict orders to keep an eye on her.

"So, dad didn't want to come?" I asked, leaning into her to whisper. "Couldn't take the time to see me himself?"

"No," Aeis answered, shaking her head, her dark hair falling over her shoulder. "I asked to come. Actually, when I got your request, the only way I could assure him that it wasn't some silly cause was for me to go myself. That way if it did end up being a joke, I was the one to take the blame."

"Good ole dad." I sighed. "He'll do whatever it takes to make sure he never takes the blame. What a leader."

"Maya, stop it." She nudged me in the side. "You know why he wouldn't believe you. Remember the incident when you were thirteen?"

I pressed my lips together tightly. "That's not even the same thing. How was I supposed to know the spies I thought I saw were really night guards training?"

Raiden snickered, and I shot a glare behind me. He sent me a wink, making me smile slightly.

"So, can we not talk about dad for once?" Aeis clutched my arm tightly. I had a feeling that things were not all good and well with my sister and father. Knowing him, he probably was doing what he usually did, running his mouth without any care for who he might hurt.

"Alright," I agreed as we approached the dining hall. "This is where we eat our meals and where Jack made a huge scene and banished his ex-girlfriend for being a raging bitch."

Aeis gasped, and Jack made a rude noise.

"I did not make a scene." Jack clicked his tongue and then crossed his arms over his chest. "It is part of the tradition to cast someone aside publicly. If I had done it in private, I would have been seen as a coward."

"Fine, fine." I let him have that one. Though I thought it was stupid.

"And this" - Raiden shoved his way in front of us with a wave of his hand - "is also where Maya flirted her way into the cook's good graces when she offended his famous raspberry tarts because of her pregnancy cravings."

"Really?" I arched a brow. "You're still on that?"

"Yes." Raiden stared me down. "You've never fluttered your lashes at me for anything."

Oh, God. What a child.

I sighed dramatically and threw a hand up. I released Aeis and took a deep breath. I clasped my hands together in front of me and fluttered my lashes more than I ever had in my entire life. "Please, Raiden forgive me for stooping so low to use my feminine wiles on Carl. I was only thinking of the welfare of the triplets."

Raiden's grin stretched across his lips and broke my pouty face. We broke into giggles just as Aeis grabbed my arm, pulling me back to her.

"Hold on a second, triplets?" she glanced down at my stomach and then back to my face. "When were you going to tell me this?"

Still laughing, I wiped the side of my eye. "Uh,

now?" When she didn't seem happy by that, I added, "We just found out ourselves, and you just got here. Besides, I'm still getting used to the idea."

The way her brow furrowed and the hurt in her eyes told me there was more to her displeasure than my omission. She wasn't upset with me for not telling her I was having triplets. This had to do with something else, something more personal. Suddenly, I felt like a huge ass.

"Guys," I said, turning to Jack and Raiden. "Could you give us a moment? I'll catch up with you at the training grounds in a little while."

Raiden and Jack exchanged a look, and then each gave me a kiss on the cheek before leaving. When they were gone, I took Aeis by the hand and brought her over to an empty table. A maid walked by, and I asked her for some tea. "Carl will know what I mean."

Turning back to my sister, I held her hand tightly. "I'm sorry, Aeis. I hope I didn't seem boastful about my pregnancy. I know this must be hard for you."

Aeis swallowed and blinked several times. "No, I'm the one who should be sorry. I'm happy for you, I really am." She left out a heavy breath. "It's just hard sometimes. I've always wanted a child.

Thought I'd have one by now and then turns out that's not in the cards for me." I squeezed her hand, urging her to continue. "Then here you are, pregnant not with one baby but three. Like, how is that fair?" She hung her head shamefully.

"Aeis, do not even feel guilty about this." I thanked the maid when she sat down our cups. The herbal tea had been one of my only drinks for the last few weeks, and I hoped it would help calm Aeis as it calmed me. "I would feel the same way if I were in your position."

"But you're not in my position." Aeis stared at me. "You have three wonderful guys who love you, babies on the way, and the whole of Western Waesigar waiting for you to take the throne."

"Okay." I leaned my head from side to side. "So, the first two are right but the last bit? I doubt it. You and I both know me getting pregnant is just a failsafe for if dad ever dies. If." I stared her down, hoping to crack a smile. "We both know he's too stubborn to ever croak, no matter how many times we wish it."

Aeis's lips quirked up at the edges.

"There it is." I poked at her with a grin. "There's that smile. Now, why don't you stop focusing on what you don't have and what you do?"

Her brow furrowed in confusion. "Three nieces or nephews to spoil rotten. Well …" I took another drink of my cup. "One is a girl for sure. The seer said so. The other two are still up in the air. I can just hope they come out before they kill me or someone else with their wacky new powers."

"Powers?"

"Oh yeah," I grimaced, wishing I hadn't said anything. I was trying to make her feel better, not brag more about my powerful embryos. "Apparently, babies channeling their powers through their mothers is a thing." I tried to downplay their abilities, so it didn't seem so much like I was shoving it in her face.

Aeis didn't get upset like I thought she would. She seemed curious. At least that was better than feeling sorry for herself.

"Anyway," I continued, not elaborating on the powers, "while we wait for Firestar to come back with a yay or nay from his father, the guys are supposed to help me channel those powers safely. I knocked the power out last night and let me tell you, no one wants me to be out of control of these powers less than me."

"So, what should my men and I do while we wait? Father won't be too happy about me hanging around doing nothing with his army." Aeis crossed her arms over her chest, a displeased scowl on her face.

I opened my mouth to tell her exactly what I thought Father could do with his impatient army when two people that made me grin came into the dining room. A wicked idea came to mind, and I had no doubt it showed on my face.

"What?" Aeis asked following my eyes to the two delicious pieces of man meat coming toward us.

"Aeis," I grinned coyly. "Have you met Raiden's brothers? His twin single brothers." A flush spread across my sister's face and down her neck, as she swallowed visibly. This was going to be fun.

8

"We shouldn't be doing this right now," Jack reminded me again even as I backed him up into the bedroom.

I licked my lips hungrily, my eyes scanning over his form. "You know I can't control when my hormones act up. And right this very second, they want nothing more than to taste every inch of you."

Jack's gaze turned dark, and the evidence of his desire pressed against the line of his pants. "While I would love to give into your every whim, we're supposed to be training."

Sashaying across the room, I began to undo the buttons of my shirt, my eyes trained on his the entire time. Shrugging out of my shirt, I let it fall to the floor. I stood there, my chest still encased in my bra with his heated gaze on me. It gave me the incentive I needed to slide my thumbs beneath the top of my pants and drop them to the floor.

Kicking them to the side, I played with the straps of my bra as I walked toward him. I pressed myself against the front of his chest, my fingers pulling down the straps and then unsnapping the back, leaving it so that the only thing keeping it up was Jack's chest.

I trailed my fingers along the line of the neck of his shirt, his head angling to the side allowing me to explore him fully. I reached up on my tiptoes and traced my tongue along the line of his jugular. I bit down slightly, making him groan, his hands gripping onto my hips.

"Jack," I cooed in his ear. "Sweet Jack. You wouldn't leave your mate to suffer on her own, now would you?" I rubbed against him in a circular pattern, making sure to brush against the front of his pants as much as possible.

He was silent for a moment, the only sound in the room was his labored breathing. Then, by some miracle, his hands dropped to my butt, cupping them as he pulled me tightly against him. I shifted my arms and moved back enough to let my bra fall to the ground, leaving me bare against him.

"Fuck it," Jack growled, lowering his mouth to mine, fiercely ravaging my lips. My hands laced into his hair, tugging him down closer as I lifted my leg to wrap around his thigh.

Grabbing me beneath my thighs, he lifted me up into his arms and turned us, laying us down on the bed behind me. I fell on the bed with a poof, the bed sinking in beneath me. Jack left my mouth and dragged his lips along my neck and down to my chest. Taking my breasts in both hands, he pressed them together before kissing them each in turn.

Licking and sucking on the tips, he had me begging for more by the time he continued his trek down my body. He hovered over my stomach, taking special care to lay a kiss on it before his fingers curled underneath the sides of my panties. Without warning, he ripped them off, the action burning against my skin before he tossed them to the side.

Before I could complain about him ruining one of my only good pair of underwear, his mouth covered my pulsing bundle of nerves. I gasped, my back arching off the bed as he nipped and sucked me into his mouth.

Barely able to catch my breath from the intensity of it all, I gripped the bedding beneath me, balling it into my fists. My toes curled under and I dragged them along the back of Jack, my heels digging into him. If it bothered him, he didn't say, but he did slip a finger inside me, rubbing from the inside and out.

"Jack, I'm about to …" My voice trailed off as my body grew hot and stars exploded behind my eyes.

I didn't have a chance to revel in my release before Jack jerked back and shouted, "Fire!"

"Huh? What?" I asked, still a bit incoherent. I followed Jack's eyes, his finger pointing at the bed next to us. There was indeed an actual fire next to me on the bed. How had I missed that? Oh, yeah, I was in the middle of orgasming.

"Did I do that?" I asked as I backed off the bed. Jack used his magic, ice coming out of his hand and extinguishing the fire before it could spread. Unfortunately, the bedding was ruined.

"It would seem your powers are becoming more unpredictable." Jack's brows furrowed a thoughtful expression on his face. He started to say something else, but I put my hand up with a warning look.

"Don't."

"What?" Jack raised a brow.

"Don't tell me I told you so because I already

know." I dragged my hand through my hair and sighed. "Training above sex. I never thought I'd have to make that rule. But hey!" I grinned at him. "At least I got off."

Jack cast his gaze to the sky before shaking his head. "Come, let's go to the library. There might be something there we can find to help you train."

"Yeah, because nothing is sexy about a library," I said sarcastically as I dug around for some new underwear.

"You find libraries arousing?" Jack asked, surprise in his voice.

I snorted and dragged my pants and shirt on. "I find the sight of you eating arousing right now, but libraries have always been something I've enjoyed. Besides, fucking against a bookshelf?" I wagged my eyebrows at him. "So hot."

Jack shook his head again and ushered me out of the room. "I'll have to keep that in mind, but after we get your powers under control."

"Whatever you say, sensei." When Jack just looked at me curiously, I waved him off. "Never mind. Let's go."

We walked down the hall in silence, me thinking about what had just happened, Jack thinking about God only knew what. Probably about the hard on I'd left him with. Though the prospect of catching on fire might have been enough to kill that wood.

"Hey," Raiden called out to us as we passed the dining hall. He had a raspberry tart in one hand with most of it already gone. "I thought you were going for a little one-on-one time?"

My mouth twisted into a grimace. "It was interrupted by the reminder that I should be training."

Raiden glanced to Jack. "How'd you convince her of that?"

"Oh, I didn't. I fully gave into her feminine wiles."

Raiden chuckled at Jack's answer. "So, she decided that for herself?" Raiden shook his head in disbelief. "That doesn't seem likely."

"I caught the bed on fire, okay?" I snapped, stomping past him and to the library just down the hall.

"Wait, what?" Raiden asked, running down the hall after me.

The moment I stepped into the library I caught sight of my sister and the twins sitting at a table together. "Shh!" I held my hand up and then ducked behind a nearby bookshelf, gesturing for the guys to follow.

"Is that my brothers?" Raiden asked, his interest in my incident thankfully forgotten.

"Yep," I nodded. "And my sister."

"I do not think this is appropriate," Jack said, moving in beside us..

"Shh, they'll hear you." I waved him off as I tried to get a better look at my sister and the twins between the books on the shelf beside us. They sat in the library chatting about something or another. I couldn't really make out what they were saying, but Aeis kept laughing and brushing her hair behind her ear, a sure sign she was into them.

Ever since I'd introduced them and saw the instant attraction, I'd done my best to put them together as much as possible. Sitting next to each other at meals. A tour of the village. Even sparring when I knew the twins would be on the training grounds. I'd never been one for matchmaking but seeing my sister so depressed gave me a need for nothing else but to see her happy. The twins could make her happy.

"I'm just saying that we should be training and not spying on your sister. She is a grown woman and can find her own mates."

I pursed my lips and shot Jack a look.

"Lighten up, Jack ole boy. We have plenty of

time to train. Besides, my brothers need a woman like Aeis to tame their wild ways." Raiden nudged Jack with a grin, trying to get a better look himself.

"You mean, how I've tamed you?" I cocked a brow. He winked at me, and I rolled my eyes, turning back to the scene before us. "You overestimate my sister's abilities to tame a man. The last one didn't go very well for her, but I'm hoping your brothers will help her not be so serious. She needs a bit of fun, after all she's gone through."

"I agree, of course." Jack placed a hand on my waist, his voice low beside my ear. "If I had any siblings, I would want to make sure they were happy as well, but do you think right now is the time to worry about that? We're on the brink of war and need to be preparing for the upcoming battle."

Twisting around so that I faced Jack, I pressed my chest against him. Looking up at him beneath my lashed, I licked my lips, making my voice go low and husky. "And if I said I wanted you to take me right here on the bookshelf, would you insist we go back to training?"

Jack swallowed visibly, the heat in his eyes making my nipples harden. "I would say …" He leaned down so his mouth hovered over mine and I inched up on my toes. "Train first, fuck later."

I dropped back onto my heels and pouted.

Raiden chuckled and shook his head. "You are a better man than me, Jack. I wouldn't have hesitated to pound our lovely mate into oblivion no matter who would hear us."

I pressed my thighs together at the visual, my heat slick with need. My gaze turned to Raiden, and I trailed my fingers along his chest. "Well, I'm not dead set on who does it."

Raiden grinned at me wolfishly, his hand covering my own. Unfortunately, before he could make good on his word, Jack stepped between us. "Hey, come on now, you passed," Raiden said with a frown.

"As much as I would love to let you exploit our mate, I would remind you of the incident that just occurred in the bedroom." Jack raised a knowing brow, and both Raiden and I slumped in defeat.

I'd been trying my best to forget about this morning, but of course, Jack had to bring it up. Though, he had a point. I really shouldn't be having sex with so many flammable objects. Or beds. Or walls. Really anywhere until I got my powers under control.

"I'm sad to say he's right." I huffed and crossed my arms over my chest. "I don't want to have to explain to Lord Fafnir why I burned down his library like I had to explain this morning with the bed covers." The memory of the bed catching on fire as I climaxed was fresh in my mind now. It was bad enough the babies made me a walking time bomb, now I couldn't even get my freak on without worry about blowing up something.

A smug grin on Jack's face he laced his fingers in front of him. "Should we adjourn to the training grounds now? Or did you want to continue to spy on your sister a bit more?"

I glanced between the books toward where my sister and the twins sat, but they were gone. Brow furrowed, I searched the library for where they could have gone until I felt a tap on my shoulder. Frozen in place, I took a moment to put a glowing smile on my lips before turning around. Aeis stood behind me with the twins in tow, curious looks covered their faces while Aeis just looked annoyed.

"Aeis! What a lovely surprise." I pulled her into my arms for a tight hug. "I didn't know you liked the library. The guys and I were just looking for some books on …" I squinted at the books on the shelf next to me. "Ice fishing."

"Ice fishing?" my sister repeated, her hands on

her hips with a disbelieving look on her face. "I didn't know you liked to fish."

"Oh, yeah. The guys and I love fishing, isn't that right?" I chuckled nervously, glancing back at Raiden and Jack for help, but they remained silent, amusement glittering in their eyes.

"You must be the fisher, because Raiden couldn't catch a fish a day in his life." Fujin nudged Raijin with a snicker.

Raiden pushed forward and pointed a finger at Fujin. "I'll have you know, I'm a great fisherman. I caught plenty of fish for us while we traveled around, didn't I?" He looked to me for approval. I should have left him high and dry like he and Jack had done me, it would serve him right.

"Oh yeah, Raiden's a great fisherman." I nodded my head a bit too enthusiastically. "In fact, it was Jack here who told us we should try ice fishing." I clapped a hand on Jack's arm, giving it a tight squeeze. "Said it would help me relax a bit."

Raijin grinned mischievously. "You mean cool off, right?"

I frowned. "No, why would I need to do that?"

"Well, we heard someone who will remain nameless destroyed an entire bed set because things got a bit too hot in the bedroom," Aeis smirked, and my eyes narrowed.

"It's not funny," I snapped, my face heating up and my hands balling into fists. "And how the hell did you find out about that so fast?"

"You would be surprised how fast gossip can spring to life around here, Maya, and you have to admit, it's a little funny." Jack ran a hand down my back in a soothing manner. "Remember to breathe."

His low reminder made me force my hands to relax and take a deep breath. When I let it out, all the building heat slowly released with it. I shook my head slightly and sighed.

"I'm sorry, it's getting increasingly harder to hold my temper. I can tell you, I'll never get on to Firestar again for being a hothead. I understand now what it's like to have this much balled-up energy inside of you on a daily basis. It's overwhelming." I gestured at my chest, earning me a sympathetic nod from everyone.

"Speaking of Firestar," my sister started, "have you heard from him lately? It's been a few days now since I've arrived, and I would imagine he'd have made it home by now."

Aeis had a point. Firestar had left several days

before Aeis had arrived, he should have arrived by now. The fact that we hadn't heard anything from him was troubling. More so for the fact that he'd gone alone.

"We haven't heard anything." I glanced at Jack and Raiden for confirmation, and they shook their heads. "Do you think something may have happened to him?" As I asked, panic began to well up inside of me. I knew it was a bad idea for Firestar to go alone. I'd told him and everyone. I had even felt something bad would happen. Now, I feared it had.

"I'm sure he's fine." Raiden placed a hand on my shoulder, drawing my eyes to him. "He probably just got delayed or forgot to send word back."

"Yes, I'm sure that's it," Jack agreed, closing in on my other side, the hand on my back moving in soothing circles. "But why don't we send a message to the South and find out for sure?"

I nodded slightly, letting them lead me out of the library. My sister and the twins followed, but I didn't really notice. I was too preoccupied with what might have happened to Firestar. Was he alright? Was he even still alive? And finally, why did I ever agree to let him go alone?

My mind reeled as Jack penned the note to

Firestar and gave it to a passing servant to be sent on the fastest messenger bird they had. Even with the fastest bird, it would still take a few days to get a response and waiting would be torture.

"I don't know if I can do this," I whispered, sitting on the edge of my bed a few feet from Jack and Raiden discussing our next move in front of me. My words interrupted their plans, and they both sat beside me.

"Maya," Jack said softly, taking my hand in his. His thumb moved along the top of my hand, sending pleasant tingles through it. I tried to focus on it and not the hollow feeling in my chest. "Everything will be fine, I promise."

"Can you though?" I glanced up from our joint hands. "Can you really promise me everything will be fine? That Firestar isn't dead or worse? Because right now I can't see it. Since I came back from Earth, everything has been one disaster after another."

"Now, that's not true." Raiden brushed a hair away from my face. "There have been some good times too."

"But everything that's happening is because of me," I countered, my eyes welling up with tears. "First, Firestar's men betray him. Then your mother betrays you. And I don't even want to get started on the whole Gretchen scenario." I paused and then remembered something. "And Ned! My favorite cousin in the entire world has turned into a rotten dirty murderer. Now tell me how my coming back was a good thing?" I let out a bitter laugh. "My sister isn't the one who's cursed, it's me."

The guys were quiet for a few moments, and the sinking feeling started to overwhelm me. They couldn't even tell me I was wrong. They knew it as much as I did. Everything horrible that has happened has been because of me. I should have just stayed on Earth. I could have helped Ryan finish making *Waesigar 2* and just daydreamed about the day I'd come back. Though, I'd have known it never would happen. It had been simpler then. Better.

"Maya," Jack said my name once more, his hand cupping my face, turning it to look at him. "It's true. Those things happened, and they happened because of you." I opened my mouth to snap at him, but he shook his head. "But none of those things were your fault. You didn't make them do what they did. Nor did you force me to leave Gretchen to be with you, which I will admit was the best decision I ever made." His pale eyes locked with mine making sure I saw how serious he was.

"He's right," Raiden said, his hand caressing my arm. "My mother was corrupt long before you got there. You only made me see what she'd been hiding. Which I'm grateful for."

"But I ruined your family."

"No," Raiden shook his head. "You gave me a new one." He placed his hand on my stomach with a small smile. "And I feel blessed every day to have you and our babies. Even Jack and Firestar." He cracked a grin over my head, and I felt Jack huff. "They are a part of me now as much as you are. I know that as long as I have you all, everything will be fine. More than fine, great."

"But what about—"

"What nothing," Jack interrupted me. "I could list my transgressions until you looked at me like I was a stranger, but that would not change anything. We are in this together. For better or worse."

"Fatness and not." Jack and I shot Raiden a look, but he only chuckled. "What I think we are saying is that we love you, and no matter what happens, that won't change."

"Right." Jack nodded and pulled me into his arms, my face pressed against his chest, the beat of his heart calming me. "We will always be here for you, and if something did happen to Firestar, we would be there for that too."

"To save his ass, of course," Raiden added, striking a silly fighting pose that belonged in a cartoon and not in real life. But it made me smile, which was what I needed.

"See?" Jack said and kissed my forehead. "We're not going anywhere."

I sagged into his arms, letting him hold me, Raiden closing in on my other side. I rubbed my face into Jack's chest, inhaling deeply. Raiden's hand stroked my thigh, causing zings of pleasure to my core. Jack stiffened beneath me, and Raiden's hand moved higher, teasing the crease of my thighs. I leaned my head up as Jack moved his down. Our lips barely brushed when the door burst open.

Jumping in place, we jerked away from each other as if we were teenagers getting caught making out in our parent's house, which I guess we were. Raijin stood in the doorway, his chest heaving, and worry etched on his face. Fujin came crowding in after him, a matching look of concern in his eyes.

"What is it?" I asked, stepping away from Raiden and Jack. My eyes drifted from their faces to the paper clutched in Raijin's hand. "Is that …?" I took a half step forward and then another until I was standing before them, my hand outreached.

"It's a message from Lord Amun," Raijin explained as I hurried to open the note. As my mind processed the words, everything that Jack and Raiden had said to calm me went out the window.

"What does it say?" Raiden asked, and I could feel the anxiety in his words because it was rampaging through me.

"Firestar never made it to the South," I murmured not quite believing it. "In fact, he never even made it to their borders." I met Jack and Raiden's gaze all the air slipping from me. "Firestar's missing."

9

———

Raiden took the note from my hand, and I let him without a word. My mind reeled. There were so many possibilities of what could have happened to Firestar.

There were plenty of people who would love to see Firestar dead, almost as many as those after me. If he didn't even hit the border, there's a high chance that Lady Nariko's men found him, or even the men that had betrayed him before. They could have been watching the border, waiting for just this opportunity and we'd given it to them.

The guys were talking about something, but I couldn't hear them over the panicked beating of my heart. My feet moved on their own, my hands ripped open my dresser drawer, and I was pulling things from it without a mind for what I was doing. I could hear some muffled conversation behind me, someone saying my name, but I didn't answer. I had to move. I had to find Firestar.

"Maya," I vaguely recognized Jack's voice near me, but I waved him off. I grabbed the bottomless bag the twins had given us and shoved the clothes I'd pulled out into it. Jack said my name again, but this time his hand latched onto mine pulling me around to face him, my hands still full of clothes. "Maya, what are you doing?"

"I'm going to find Firestar, what does it look like?" I jerked away from him and turned back to my bag. Jack sighed and rubbed a hand over his face. Raiden left his brothers and moved in on the other side of me. I forced myself to ignore both of them as I continued to pack my bag.

"Maya, sweetheart." Raiden reached out and took the bag from my hand. Or tried to. I clutched it in my hand, tugging it back toward me. "You can't go off by yourself."

"Then come with me," I snapped back, jerking the bag out of his hands. "It'll be easier to find him with more people."

Raiden huffed and looked at Jack over my shoulder. Jack placed his hand on my shoulder, turning me slightly toward him. I glowered at him, my patience wearing thin. "Think about this for a moment, we do not know where Firestar even is, and do you think that it is wise for you to go chasing after him in your condition?"

"I'm pregnant, not a cripple!" I could feel my face heating up, and I forced myself to calm down before I blew something up. My hands tightened on the bag, and I growled out a breath. "I'm more than capable of taking care of myself and our babies."

"I know that," Raiden argued, his hand on my arm, "but you shouldn't put yourself into these situations on purpose. If you were the one who was captured, that would be one thing, but we have plenty of men who are waiting just outside who could and would die to protect you."

"But it's Firestar," I whimpered, my eyes burning. "He wouldn't even be in this position if not for me."

"First, off," Jack growled, impatience in his voice, "none of us are your responsibility. We are here because we want to be, not because you or anyone else made us. And that'll be enough of the self-pity and blame." I opened my mouth to argue, but he held his hand up. "The next time I hear anything like that out of your mouth, I will put you across my knee."

My mouth dropped open at the implications of Jack's words. I would have expected that kind of talk from Raiden or Firestar, but Jack? He had never really been the type.

"But what am I going to do waiting around here? I'll go out of my mind."

Jack looked pointedly at my stomach. "I could think of three things that could keep you busy."

My hand went to the swell of my belly, and I remembered specifically why I hadn't gone with him in the first place. As much as I hated to admit it, they were right. Chasing down Firestar wasn't the best of ideas. If we had an idea of where he was, it would make more sense to go after him personally. Since we were in the dark, well, it was hard for me to argue their point, no matter how much I wanted to go after him.

My feelings were in such a state of chaos, I had a hard time picking one out from the other. Anger. Worry. Desperation. Love. Sometimes, I just wished I could shut them all down. Have a clear head for once.

As if some genie had heard my internal wish, a numb feeling started to spread from my center and down my arms. I let the emptiness take over, taking solace in the nothing. For one of the first times in a long time, I felt completely at ease. A crackling jerked me out of my serenity and made me glance down. My hands were cold, and everywhere my fingers touched, the bag in my hand froze over. Shocked, I dropped the bag promptly. It fell to the ground, the ice that had begun to form on the side of it breaking into shards on the ground.

I really needed to get a handle on these powers.

"See?" Raiden took my hands in his with a soft expression. "You should stay here and train. Get control of your abilities and keep our babies safe."

"But what about Firestar?" I shook my head, unable to just let it go. "I can't just leave him to die."

"And we won't," Jack reassured me, pulling me into his arms. "In fact, Raiden and I will go after him make sure he's safe."

"And if he's not?" I pushed away from his embrace, my hands wringing in front of me. "What if he's dead? Or worse?"

Raiden barked a laugh. "I highly doubt that stubborn ass is dead."

Jack shot Raiden a chastising look. "That's enough of that." He glanced back at the twins who stood awkwardly waiting at the doorway, concern etched on both of their faces. "Can we send some scouts out to see if we can find out anything about where Firestar might have gone? Where he was last seen?"

Raijin nodded. "I'm sure that won't be a problem. Aeis brought some of the best trackers in the West with her rather large army." The grin on his lips made me wonder if that's all that Aeis had divulged to the two of them.

The twins took off to find Aeis or the trackers, I wasn't sure which. They hadn't been too clear, and I was too worried about Firestar to care. I pushed out from between Jack and Raiden, needing some space to think. I paced the floor, beating my fist against my hand. "How long do you think it will take?" I asked, anxiety making me twitch.

"To find Firestar?" Raiden cocked his head to the side and then shrugged. "Who knows. Could take hours or even days. Hell, maybe even weeks-ouch!" Raiden glared at Jack who had smacked him on the chest. Jack gave him a warning look which made Raiden clear his throat and scratch his ear. "Uh, I mean, I'm sure it will be fine. Like my brother said, your sister brought some of the best trackers in your region. They'll find out what happened to him in no time."

I pursed my lips, not believing him for one moment. I wasn't naïve, I knew that the longer it took to find Firestar the less likely of a chance he would be found alive. That was a possibility that I couldn't grasp. I needed Firestar. His child needed him. I knew we'd be alright if something happened to him, I had Jack and Raiden, but it wouldn't be the same. I'd always feel like a part of me was missing. The same way I'd felt when he left the first time.

Chewing on my nail, I tried to force down all the awful things that my mind played through my mind of what could have happened to Firestar. Could they be torturing him right now? For fun or for information? Maybe he was being held hostage to get to me? My hand went to my stomach, and my heart jumped into my throat. Or maybe to get to our baby?

"Maya." Jack's soothing tone caught my attention. "Whatever you are thinking, you need to stop." His words made me stop pacing, and I looked up to meet his eyes, but they weren't on me, they were on my hands. I glanced down quickly and frowned when I saw them glowing yellow-white, like Raiden's powers.

Crap.

I closed my eyes and took a deep breath before letting it out slowly. Opening my eyes, I was happy to see the power had dissipated. I dragged my hands through my hair and sat down on the side of my bed. "What are we going to do?"

"I don't know about this guy," Raiden pointed a thumb at Jack and then wandered over to me. "But I plan on taking my woman down to the kitchen and stuffing her with so much food, she won't be worrying about anything but how full she is." He leaned forward until our faces were close to each other, his hands on either side of me.

Pushing him away with a laugh, I shook my head. "As much as I'd love that, I can't think about food right now. Not while Firestar is missing."

Jack frowned and stepped beside us. "You cannot neglect yourself because of this. You have others to care for."

"I know, I know." I fluttered my hand in the air and sighed. "I'll eat something, just not right now. Right now, I need to …" My voice trailed off, my brow furrowing as I remembered something.

"Need to what?" Raiden asked, moving away

from me slightly.

I put my hand up to stop him from talking as I tried to recall all of last night's dream. Or what I'd thought was a dream. The beginning for sure had been one but the rest. The bag being pulled over my head, the gag in my mouth, that had been different. Too real to be a dream.

"Maya," Jack said, his head tilting to the side making his hair cascade over his shoulders. I couldn't appreciate the beauty of it though, I was too caught up in remembering.

"I think I had a vision last night," I told them finally.

"A vision?" Raiden asked and then met Jack's eyes before turning back to me. "What kind of vision?"

I shook my head. "I don't know. It didn't start out as a vision. I'd been having a nightmare about Gretchen." When I said her name, Jack tensed, but I waved him off. "Then it changed."

"Changed how?" Jack asked, curiosity in his strained gaze.

"I was being taken away. Someone – no, more than one person - grabbed me. I didn't see who they were. They put a bag over my head, it smelled like …" I paused and closed my eyes trying to recall the smell of it. "Dirt. The bag smelled of dirt and trees. I remember it vividly, the bag made me claustrophobic. It was hard to breathe through it and the gag."

"Maybe it was just a dream." Raiden stroked my arms, trying to reassure me.

"No," I shook my head. "It wasn't. I've had visions before."

"You have? Why didn't you tell us?" Jack seemed offended by my lack of sharing, but I didn't apologize.

"I wasn't sure it was real. I thought it might be a fluke or something that seer did to me." I shifted on the bed and focused on what happened before. "During the hunt, when you were trying to find me." I waited for them to nod that they understood before continuing. "I had a dream. You were arguing about my going off on my own. I saw through Jack's eyes. I could feel how upset you felt about keeping things from me. That's why it was easy for me to forgive you." I offered Jack a soft smile, knowing he still felt guilty about the whole Gretchen ordeal. "Plus, Raiden and Firestar were giving you enough shit about it. Me piling in on you wasn't going to help much."

"I still say you should have beaten him up for

that one. I would have helped," Raiden grinned cheekily at me, earning him a snort from Jack.

"Anyway," I continued, ignoring Raiden's attempt to start something, "you guys found the blood from where Gretchen clawed me by the river, and that's it. I didn't get any more than that."

The guys were quiet for a moment, as if really letting my words sink in. Really, I wouldn't blame them if they were upset at me for leaving this new ability out, but I hadn't been sure it was real, and not just my overactive imagination or some pregnancy dream cooked up by the babies. We all knew they were chock full of surprises. Who knew if this wasn't another one of theirs?

Eventually, Jack was the one who broke the silence. "So, you are saying that you are having visions of things happening to us?" He circled his finger between him and Raiden. "No one else?"

I shook my head. "No, I've only had dreams of your guys, no one else. Do you think it's the babies? Or maybe it's our bond?" I gave a nervous chuckle. "I don't know about you, but I'm fine with how close we are now. I don't need to be inside of your heads all the time."

"Thank God for that." Raiden grinned causing me to frown, and he quickly added, "I think about sex a lot." My eyes narrowed, and he smirked, his brows wagging. "With you. In all manner of places."

I puffed out a laugh and shoved his shoulder. "Pervert."

Jack didn't bother commenting on Raiden's admission but stroked his jaw in thought. "You said you smelled dirt and trees?" I nodded. "Anything else you can tell us?"

I opened my mouth to say no but then stopped. There was something else. I just wasn't sure if I was right or not. "They put me in some kind of vehicle. Maybe a carriage?"

"Then there would be tracks of some sort, right?" Raiden provided. "If they hadn't been smart enough to cover it up, then they should still be there. He hasn't been gone long."

"But if it was here, then the recent snow might have covered it." Jack gestured out the window.

"It wasn't cold," I remembered suddenly. "I mean not like this cold. Though Firestar's a virtual furnace, I don't remember it being more of a balmy in-between?" I said, unsure of my description. "Where could that be?"

Jack and Raiden exchanged a look and then said at the same time. "The unaligned."

10

If I thought I was anxious before, waiting for Firestar to send word about his father's decision, waiting to find out where he might be was even worse. I sat in the dining room with three empty cups of tea in front of me and my hands were still shaking.

"Deep breaths," Jack reminded me for the millionth time, and I was so close to punching him in the throat. It'd make me feel better but only for a second, and then I'd regret it. Instead of giving into my baser urges, I did as he suggested.

Breathe in, breathe out. After another deep breath, I let it out with a growl. "This is utter bullshit. We should be out looking for him, not waiting for someone else to do it."

"Maya! Watch your mouth." The way Aeis said my name reminded me of our mother which irritated me even more.

"Aeis!" I quipped back with an eye roll. "You're not the one with someone in danger. Don't lecture me. Your mouth is worse than mine at times."

"N-no … it's not." She stuttered and flushed beet red, her eyes darting over to the twins who only grinned in response.

"That's okay." Fujin smirked and draped an arm over the back of Aeis's chair. "I like a dirty mouth." His words made Aeis's face turned even redder, and I squirmed in my seat. It was one thing to play matchmaker, but it was another completely to see them flirting like that.

"Dude, gross." Raiden made a face and then gestured at his plate. "I'm eating. Just cause you and Raijin like to share doesn't mean I want to be in on it. I have no desire to know anything about your sex life."

"You … you like to share?" Aeis barely got the words out her eyes going wide. My sister had been pledged to someone before, a really great guy that we all thought would be a great leader. Then he found out she was barren and took off for greater vaginas. Fucking idiot. Safe to say my sister hasn't had much luck in the man department since that. I definitely couldn't see her in any kind of threesome like I'd done with Raiden and Jack.

The way she kept shifting in her seat told me she wasn't completely unopposed to the idea. Ugh. Now, I lost my appetite.

"What's wrong?" Carl asked suddenly, having appeared next to our table. "Do you not like the tea?"

My eyes widened, and I grabbed my cup, bringing it to my mouth. "No, no. I love the tea thank you. We were just talking about something unpleasant, is all."

Carl relaxed, seeming pacified for now. "Good, I made tonight's meal especially with you in mind. No heavy seasoning or syrups. Just like you specified."

"Which I appreciate greatly." I nodded, even though I found the meal tasteless and bland.

To add to the façade, I picked up my fork and scooped up a spoonful of some kind of vegetable mash and shoved it into my mouth. I chewed it quickly and swallowed with a pained grin. After Carl left, I took another drink of my tea to wash down the remainder of the mash stuck to my throat. A mixture of chuckles caused me to glance up.

"You're a horrible liar," Raiden muttered, leaning into me with another laugh.

Pushing him away with my elbow, I wasn't able to hide the grin on my lips. The rest of the table had equally amused expressions. Not wanting to be the butt of the joke any longer, I scooped up more of the mash and flicked it at Raiden. It hit him on the side of the face with a smack, not sticking but sliding down his cheek.

The table erupted in laughter. Even Jack let out a chuckle or two. I knew that I'd pay for this later, but right now the look on Raiden's face was worth it.

"Did you just …?" Raiden's voice trailed off as if not quite believing what happened. He reached up and brushed the remainder of the mash off the side of his face and looked at me with a gaping mouth.

I tried to stifle a laugh but ended up snorting instead. Clamping a hand over my mouth didn't help cover the giggles that forced their way out.

"You're gonna pay for that." Raiden's voice came out low and dangerous, the kind of voice he used when we were in the bedroom. My heart quickened, and for once, it had nothing to do with Firestar's disappearance and everything to do with Raiden.

I smiled coyly as I slipped another spoonful into my mouth, hoping it looked sexy. It must have worked because Raiden's eyes darkened, and his hand landed on my inner thigh. I licked my lips and swallowed hard, need pulsating through my veins.

"I don't know about you, but I'm not hungry anymore," Raiden announced, getting to his feet. "At least, not for food." A wicked grin spread across his lips, and I didn't hesitate when he held his hand out to me.

"Me either," I couldn't get out fast enough, shooting a look around the table. What met me were knowing glances and arched brows, the former from Jack. I locked eyes with him and then glanced shyly back at Raiden who seemed to get my unspoken question. Once he shrugged his approval, I offered a hand to Jack. "Come on, I could use help with … uh … some things."

"Smooth, Maya." Raiden snickered and shook his head. "Real smooth." To the rest of the table, he nodded and grinned. "Have a good night."

Chuckling amongst themselves, the twins draped an arm each around my sister's shoulders.

Raijin whispered something in her ear, making her blush again, and then he said to us, "I think we're good."

Trying not to think of the implications that were behind those words, I let Raiden and Jack lead me out of the dining hall and toward our bedroom. It seemed to take forever to get there, and as soon as the door closed behind us, we were on each other. Hands grabbed at each other's clothes and mouths blurred together until I wasn't sure who was where.

Eventually, I found myself on my knees before Raiden, my mouth wrapped around his length. My tongue slid down the base of him at the same time my hand moved along Jack's, cupping him beneath. Raiden's hand tangled in my hair, guiding me the way he wanted it. Jack didn't need such control, he let me pull and tighten my grip on him however I liked. The contrast was strange and slightly liberating.

"Enough," Raiden gasped, his voice husky and low. I glanced up beneath my lashes to see the strain on his face and didn't stop. He tightened his grip on my hair and gave me a tug, forcing me to release him from my mouth. I grinned and licked my lips, leaning back on my heels. Jack moved out of my grasp as well, watching as I stared down Raiden.

"I think our girl needs to learn a lesson." Raiden met Jack's gaze. "A lesson about respect and thinking of others."

I stood and backed away from them, not in fear but desire. My hands gripped the edge of the bed. I slipped on it, my legs falling open wide, baring me to their hungry eyes.

For a moment, Raiden stopped talking and just stared at me, but then he seemed to remember himself. He tisked and waved his finger at me like a naughty child. "You are not being fair. This isn't about you. This is about us and how you don't seem to think we might care if you take off after Firestar and get yourself hurt. What do you think Firestar would think of that?" He raised a brow as he approached the edge of the bed. His fingers played along my ankle and then up my calf before wrapping around it. He dragged me further down the bed so that my butt barely sat on the edge.

The bed dipped beside me, and I turned my head slightly to see Jack. He shifted until he sat behind me, his hands curving over my shoulders. His front pressed against me, his hardness rubbing my lower back. I leaned into him as his mouth brushed against the side of my neck. Teeth skimmed the line of my throat at the same time as

Raiden's touched the inside of my thigh and I jerked.

"How are you feeling right now?" Raiden breathed against my hot core, his hands sliding beneath my hips. "How you feel about Firestar is how we would feel if anything happened to you. Do you understand?"

My head fell back against Jack's shoulder as Raiden's tongue lapped at my folds before pulling back, making me buck my hips. Jack's arms slipped between mine and cupped my breasts. His fingers plucked at my nipples, dragging out my need. I moaned out a plea for more but was ignored.

"Answer me," Raiden's voice rumbled between my thighs.

I swallowed, my mouth thick with desire. "Yes. Yes, I understand."

I barely had gotten the words out when Raiden's mouth closed over me. I gasped and groaned, my eyes rolling up into my head. Raiden sucked on my sensitive nub, pulling it into his mouth. My back arched, and a gurgling scream ripped from my throat. I could feel my release just on the other side of the cusp, but before I could reach it, Raiden moved away.

"No, no." I gasped, shaking my head from side to side. "I was almost there."

"I know," Raiden smiled sadly. He glanced over my shoulder, I presumed at Jack, but my desire-muddled mind couldn't care too much. They must have some kind of telepathy because they moved as one, pulling me further onto the bed and situating me so that I sat above Jack, Raiden at my back. The position was new and different. It excited me, but a small part of me hesitated, unsure.

"Shh," Raiden smoothed his hand down my back, murmuring reassurance in my ear. "It's alright." He was so close to me that I could feel his breath on my shoulder. His hand sat on my hip, and I waited to see what he'd do. Dozens of scenarios ran through my mind but what I didn't expect was for Raiden's hand to wrap around Jack in front of me.

I gasped, my mouth dropping open at the sight of him touching Jack. My eyes trailed up Jack's chest to his face, but the tension I thought I'd see there was nowhere to be seen. If anything, he seemed into it.

Huh. Who knew?

The hand on my hip shifted, lifting me up. The hand holding Jack aligned him with my center, stroking his head along my folds before Raiden urged me to sink down. The first bit of Jack stretched me, a stinging feeling that quickly turned to a dull throb. When Jack was fully seated inside of me, Raiden's fingers dipped down to trace the top of my core, soothing away some of the aches that came from someone as large as Jack.

Jack grunted, his hands finding the tops of my thighs. "Raiden."

The single word was enough for Raiden to let me move. I rocked on my knees, and Jack slowly drew out of me before I sank back down. The movement caused a deliriously delicious sensation throughout that I had to do it again and again. Soon, Jack and I had found a rhythm, our eyes firmly locked on each other. When Raiden's fingers moved further down to stroke around my entrance, I hardly noticed, but as soon as they prodded my back entrance, I froze.

"Do you want me to stop?" Raiden asked, the tip of his finger circling the puckered flesh.

I swallowed and shook my head. It wasn't like I'd never done it before, but doing it with more than one man? That would be a new experience for me. One that I wasn't sure I'd survive but wanted to find out.

Raiden's digit slid in slowly. There was a bit of resistance, but I tried to breathe through it. Jack's hands on my legs shifted up to my hips and lower back. He urged me to lean forward until my stomach brushed against his. The position made him move inside of me, and I let out a low groan.

A hand settled on the back of my neck, the pressure of Raiden's grasp telling me what he wanted me to do. I bent my knees, sinking back down onto Jack and the finger, the combination a thrilling fullness I could imagine would only be better with more. Determined to find my release, I braced myself against Jack's chest and rocked my hips once more. Once I started, I couldn't stop, I only paused when Raiden added another finger stretching me even more.

"Just breath," Raiden told me circling his fingers inside of me. Soon, I was moving again, my breath coming out in gasps and groans. "That's it, love. Just relax." Raiden moved closer to me, his length rubbing against my butt. I had a feeling I knew where this was going, and I wanted it. Oh, did I want it.

I didn't even stop when I felt an emptiness where his fingers had been before, because it was soon replaced by the head of him pressed where his hand had been before. The next rock of my hips sank him into me, and my breath caught. My tongue darted out as I met Jack's eyes. He nodded as if to say I could do this. Not that I needed the encouragement, but it was appreciated. At a snail's pace, I lowered my hips, pulling Jack and Raiden inside of me.

Stilling, I closed my eyes as I tried to get used to the fullness. If I had thought Raiden's fingers before had been great, it didn't even compare to this.

Neither of them moved or forced me to go any faster than I wanted to but even I couldn't wait any longer. I lifted myself back up and then lowered my hips. The second time was even better than the first, so much so I did it again. Jack's hands on my hips tightened and helped move me. My breathing became labored, the heat of Raiden on my back and Jack cool against my front only adding to the pleasure. I could feel my orgasm closing in on me, and for the first time, I worried I'd have a repeat of the other morning.

"It's okay," Jack said as if knowing what I was thinking. "We've got you."

My breath hitched, and I couldn't stop my release from coming. I closed my eyes and prayed I would keep it together. Jack reached it first, stilling beneath me, my own not far behind him.

An overwhelming feeling of chaos spread throughout, and I couldn't breathe. Jack's fingers pinched at my hip, making my eyes open and lock with his again. The pain helped reign in the uncontrollable feeling I had just enough to let my orgasm take me without losing it.

Raiden thrust a few more times before he too grunted and stilled behind me. He pressed his face against my back, the sticky feel of his skin not bothering me but the thought of crushing the triplets did. I shifted, gesturing for him to let me out from under him. I collapsed on the bed beside Jack, Raiden following behind me to lay on the other side.

The only sound in the room were three sets of breathing. My body tingled and ached in all the right places. I'd never felt so satisfied before in my life.

I stared up at the ceiling and then gaped, "Wow."

"Wow, indeed." Jack echoed after me, his fingertips making designs on my arm.

Raiden held my hand and brought it to his lips. "No more talk of going after Firestar."

I scoffed. "You think you can screw me into submission?"

Raiden and Jack chuckled, that male kind of laugh that meant they knew what they were capable of. It'd have made me ready for round two if I wasn't already thoroughly sexed up.

When they didn't respond, I sighed. "Fine, it's not like I could walk right now anyway." They laughed, and we settled in for the night, which I hoped wouldn't end with just sleep.

11

––––––

Several days later, I sat on the floor of my bedroom, staring down at my hand. A flame flickered in my palm, small at first and then larger as I focused harder. I molded the fire into a ball the size of a baseball.

I tossed it once and then twice in the air making it dance before me. It twisted and spiraled into a butterfly, its wings spread out in flight. Then it moved on its own, shifting into a familiar face. One I'd dreamed about for several nights now.

I sighed and stared at the silhouette. Firestar. Where are you?

The image warped again back into a ball of fire that settled on my palm. Controlling fire was much different than commanding any other element.

With earth, I didn't create it. I coaxed it and plants to do my bidding. The fire, on the other hand, couldn't be coaxed. It had to be commanded, shown who was boss.

My lips quirked up slightly. A bit like its owner. Firestar was volatile and could get out of control if not watched carefully. The rest of the elements were a bit different, no weaker than fire but a bit easier to manage.

I held up my other hand, and it began to glow softly. The light grew slowly as the low hum turned into a crackle, sparks of electricity dancing around my hand. Electricity flirted. It teased. It didn't take much to get it to do what you wanted. A promise of fun things to come was all the bargaining it took to get it to do what I wanted.

A snort slipped out. Raiden wasn't far off from the same.

It took a while for me to be able to switch between the powers with such ease. Even now, I had a hard time keeping the fire from overwhelming the electricity. I closed my hand over the fire, willing it to go down, but the heat in my hand didn't lessen. The ball of fire built up, shoving my fingers open as a large ball of flame took up most of my hand.

Taking a deep breath, I stared down the flame,

demanding it to disperse. When it didn't work, I reached inside of myself and found the cold piece of me. A gentle outstretched hand was all it needed to come forth. My arm cooled as the magic crept through my veins and settled into my palm. The fireball that had gotten a mind of its own hissed and sizzled as the ice overtook it. Soon the fire extinguished, and a ball of ice took its place. It slipped out of my hand and crashed to the floor with a loud thud.

The sound caused me to lose my concentration, and the energy in my other hand disappeared. I sighed and frowned at the ball of ice. Nudging it with my foot, I watched it roll across the floor and bump against the wall.

I leaned back until I laid on the floor. I closed my eyes and breathed in and out. Raiden and Jack had tried their best to keep me so busy enough in the bedroom not to think about Firestar at night but during the day - it was harder.

If I wasn't in the library, searching every book I could for anything on my power situation, then I was in my room practicing. I had plates piled by the door that were taken by one of the servants every once in a while. I rarely went to the dining hall anymore. Carl, though, made sure I had anything I wanted to be delivered to my room. I had a constant pot of tea on the table near the window. It had probably gone long cold by now. Not that I had drunk any of it.

I was tired of being calm.

Sometimes, I practiced in the training fields but usually by myself or with a dummy. The guys had tried to help me at first, but after the first day, they started to be available less and less. I'd have been worried had I not known they were locked up in Lord Fafnir's office all day. They saw him more than me at that point.

Of course, I wasn't allowed in the meetings. For my own good and those around me. Though I could argue that I hadn't caught anything on fire in a few days. I could even have an orgasm without worrying about the upholstery.

Unfortunately, that didn't go the same for idiot douche bags with big mouths. I really didn't like that Deric. Lord Fafnir was afraid I'd accidentally hit him with a fireball like I did Jack the other day. Believe me, if I attacked Deric, it wouldn't be an accident.

Nevertheless, here I was, practicing.

I wasn't missing out on anything really. Not the

way Raiden explained it. It was a lot of arguing and boring tactician discussions.

Should they attack from the north or to from the coast? What about the differences in magic? Would it harder for the ice dragons to fight against the electric ones? On and on it went. I'd had to stop Raiden long before he could give me the complete run down. Though I had a hard time being interested in the conversation, I still wanted to feel like I was a part of it, not just sitting on the sidelines, playing with magic.

What made it worse was that Aeis got to be in on the meetings as the head of the Western Army. That made complete sense, of course, and I shouldn't have been bitter about it, but I couldn't help it. I was tired of being cooped up in my room or on the training field, practicing like I was some adolescent learning how to control my powers for the first time. Which I guess I was, when I thought about it that way.

I blew out a hard breath and sat up. This was stupid. The scouts should have been back by now. It was worrying that we hadn't heard anything yet. Firestar couldn't have gotten far before he was taken, and there were only so many places he could be taken to.

A bubbling in my stomach made me glanced down. "You guys think so too, huh?"

"Oh no," a voice groaned from behind me, followed by a chuckle. "Please tell me you haven't broken down and started talking to yourself?"

I twisted around to see Raiden leaning against the bedroom door, a lopsided grin on his face. Grunting, I pushed myself to my knees and then to my feet.

Raiden reached out to help me just as I settled on my feet. I held onto his arm until I was steady before I turned and smacked him on the chest. "I'm not talking to myself, I'm talking to the babies."

"Oh, well, that's different," Raiden smirked, and I smacked him again. "How are my lovelies today?" He placed his hands on either side of my stomach, a soft look of adoration on his face. My heart warmed at the sight. He was going to be a great father.

"They're good, a bit gassy." I felt a series of bubbles in my stomach again and smiled as Raiden's eyes widened.

"What was that?"

"They do move, you know." I chuckled, amused by the look of terror on his face. It was like he expected them to pop out of me or something, like a cheap horror movie.

Raiden moved his hands over my stomach, a sense of wonder in his eyes. "Do they do this often?"

I shrugged and rotated my neck. "Only about every other minute. Especially, when I'm trying to sleep." I shifted away from him, so his hand dropped. "I'm afraid before too long I won't be able to sleep at all." I shifted uncomfortably. "Or fit in my clothes."

"Well, there's an easy fix for that." Raiden slipped his arms in from behind me. "We'll just have to get rid of them."

"The babies?" I jerked in his arms, my mouth dropping open. How could he even think such a thing? These were our babies. I couldn't get rid of them just because I was a little inconvenienced. So, what if I couldn't quite touch my toes anymore, and the sight of fish made me want to vomit? I wouldn't trade them for all the world.

Chuckling behind me unaware of my distress, Raiden nuzzled my neck. "No, your clothes."

"Ugh, don't do that. I thought you wanted to …" I shook my head. "Never mind." I pushed my way out of his arms and turned around. "Did you just come in here to flirt, or did you have a reason for disturbing my training?"

"Can't I do both?" He gave me a lopsided grin.

I crossed my arms over my chest. "No, and where's Jack? I thought he was with you." I angled my head to look around him, like Jack was hiding back there or something.

"He's talking to his uncle."

"When is he not?" I rolled my eyes and sighed. "Did you guys at least figure anything out?"

Tucking his hands into his pockets, Raiden rocked on his heels. His brow furrowed, and his tongue licked across his teeth. He was hiding something. Something he didn't want to tell me.

"What is it?" I stepped toward him, my chest tightening at what he might say. "Is it Firestar? Did you find him? He's dead, isn't he?" His silence was getting to me, making my mind call up all sorts of things.

"Shh, shush now." Raiden took me by the shoulders and pulled me to him. "Nothing like that. He's not dead, but he has been taken."

I jerked my head back to look up at him. "Who? Who took him?"

Raiden met my gaze and sighed. "The unaligned."

"The unaligned?" My face scrunched up. "Why would they want him?"

Raiden released me and stepped back. "From what the trackers saw, it was the guys from his old regiment. The ones who wanted him to share you." He stared me down as if trying to get me to remember.

It wasn't hard though. Everyone and their moms have wanted me to mate with them so I could give them powers. The joke was on them though, because I was pretty sure the only way they'd get it was if I wanted them back.

Not that they would believe me.

"I remember." I gulped and inclined my head. "So, what do we do now? We're going after him, right?"

"Of course, we are," Raiden reassured me. "We are gathering men as we speak to infiltrate the unaligned camp."

"Good, let's go." I started for the door, but Raiden caught my arm, stopping me. "What? Don't think that I'm staying behind, not after everything that's happened."

"Would it make a difference?" he asked. I glared at him, and he let out a bitter laugh. "I didn't think so." Dragging hand through his hair, Raiden huffed. "Lord Fafnir wants us to be diplomatic about all this. To contact the leader of the unaligned first, asking him to let Firestar go before we go charging in."

"Okay?"

"And he thinks that the best way to do that is for us to go in there … together." He circled between us with a frown.

"Is that safe?" I questioned. While I didn't want to be left behind, I wasn't sure I wanted to be in the middle of the unaligned camp either.

Nodding, Raiden took my hand. "We'll meet him in a neutral spot, and then our men will sneak in and get Firestar out in case the talks goes south."

"So, it's a setup. Won't that piss the leader off?"

Raiden snorted. "Probably, but we'll be long gone by then. Besides, he doesn't want to start a war with three out of the four regions, does he?" The grin on his face was positively lethal. I knew from the bottom of my heart, that if anyone could get Firestar out, it would be Raiden. After all, it'd be good practice for the fight to come.

12

The unaligned territory didn't really belong to them. It sat on the junction of where the four kingdoms of Waesigar meet. Technically, they were in everyone's territory. It's how they had been able to stay there for so long without one of the lords coming in to kick them out. Any action by a lord to move against the unaligned would raise the tension between that lord and the others. No one liked armies near their borders, after all.

Most of the time, the unaligned kept to themselves and didn't make waves, another reason the lords didn't find them worth the trouble. Lately, though, they'd begun to grow, and those newcomers weren't just making waves. They were making tsunamis. My father was already on the verge of sending men in to take them out, and I had no doubt the rest of the lords would follow.

Now, though, it wasn't my father or the other lords they had to worry about. It was me, one pregnant, pissed-off dragon. A volatile combination that would decide if the unaligned even existed anymore after I was through with them.

"Fix your face," Raiden whispered next to me as we headed on foot toward the meeting place. It was just off the border of the North but not completely into the unaligned compound.

"What's wrong with my face?" I snapped, already irritable from the travel. I had a hard enough time getting comfortable in a real bed, sleeping on the cold hard ground wasn't making it any easier.

"You look ready to shed blood, love." Jack touched my lower back. "We don't want to give off the wrong kind of signal before we even start the talks."

"What kind of signal would that be?" I asked with as much snark as I could muster.

"Threatening."

"They have one of my men. Of course, I'm threatening them." I glared at Jack, my face heating up so much, I knew that I would accidentally light something on fire if I didn't calm down. My fingers curled into fists, and I took deep cleansing breaths. Save the meltdown for the enemy.

"We don't know for sure that Orion sanctioned the capture," my sister reminded me with a pointed look. Aeis, along with the twins, led the group and had to glance back over her shoulder to see me, but even then, I could feel the chastising coming off her in waves. "You don't want to pick a fight with the unaligned before you even become the Lady of the West, do you?"

My jaw tightened, and I shook my head. "No, but if we find out that Orion was responsible for this, then all bets are off." I flashed my fangs, my skin crackling with power. "They will burn with the rest of them."

"Maya." My sister gave me a soft look. "You're talking about women and children. Innocents who know nothing of what has happened. You can't kill a whole group of people based on the actions of a few individuals among them."

My anger lessened, and I blew out a hard breath. "You're right. But someone will pay, and it better be with blood." I stomped forward until I passed my sister and the twins.

"Is it just me, or is she getting pissier the bigger she gets?" Fujin muttered behind me, and my head snapped to look at him.

"I heard that."

Fujin shrugged apologetically, but I'd already forgotten him, my attention turned to that of the large group standing over the hill. A dozen or so men gathered around one who, despite his simplistic dress, could not be mistaken for anything other than a lord.

It was in the way he held himself. He didn't shift or fiddle, his eyes firmly on the person who spoke to him. That was a younger man who I could only assume was his son. They were both handsome in their own way, with light brown hair and rugged features, definitely my sister's type.

"Maya." Aeis's warning voice made me realize I'd been grinning like a crazy person. "Whatever you're thinking, stop. We're here to save Firestar, remember?"

I rolled my eyes. "How can I forget? But it wouldn't hurt for you to use your feminine wiles on them. You know, soften them up a bit for us?" I smirked.

Crossing her arms over her chest, her face went red. "Why don't you?"

I gestured to my stomach with raised brows. "While I might still be sexy as all get out, I don't think they would want to get with a woman already pregnant by three other men."

Raiden and Jack let out a growl in agreement. I shot them an appreciative grin. "Besides, we don't want sex with me to be on the table. We don't want them thinking in any direction of my abilities." I did air quotes as I said it. The last time – the last two times, actually - anyone found out about my powers, they'd tried to force me into being a power horse, someone they could use and toss aside when they were done with me.

Now that I was pregnant, I wouldn't be letting anyone touch me but the three who made me this way, no matter what some seer said.

"Are you ready for this?" Jack asked, coming to stand to my right side.

I took a deep breath and let it out. "As ready as I will ever be. Are our men in position?" I kept my eyes forward on the waiting party, trying not to give away our ruse.

"They're waiting just outside the woods near where they are keeping Firestar." Raiden lined up his steps with mine on my other side.

"Good." My lips curled up, and even I knew it wasn't a pleasant grin.

"Remember, be nice." Jack's voice danced in my ears, making some of the tension in my shoulders to ease.

"I'm always nice," I shot back as we stopped before the group. Our own group consisted of me, Jack, Raiden, my sister, the twins, and two guards. We'd agreed upon only bringing a few people to this meeting to keep it from going into bloodshed. The way the men were leering at my sister and myself, I didn't see how that wouldn't happen and soon.

"Lords and ladies." Orion greeted us with a sly grin and open arms. I didn't trust him already. "I trust the trip was pleasant."

"As pleasant as can be when pregnant," I couldn't help but quip.

Orion's eyes dropped to my swollen belly barely contained in my jacket. "I apologize for any unpleasantness you might have had on your journey. My wife had a difficult pregnancy herself when she had our boy. Not so much with our daughter though. She seemed too ready to be out in the world."

The grin on his face was meant to ease me, but I didn't drop my guard.

His expression wilted slightly before he turned and placed a hand on the male's shoulder next to him confirming my suspicions. "This is Blake, my oldest. My daughter, Ellie is busy teaching the young ones some Earth nonsense and couldn't be bothered to attend."

The way he talked about his daughter told me that he expected her to learn as much as his son did about politics. That was something my own father never cared about, not until my brother died and left him with nothing but girls. Even then, he expected our mates to take care of the political aspects, not the 'weak' women. Orion's distinction made me like him a little bit more.

"We are happy to meet your acquaintance." I nodded to Blake but didn't offer my hand. Instead, I gestured toward the rest of our group. "This is my sister, Aeis. The twins are Fujin and Raijin, firstborns of the Eastern Region." The twins nodded in turn and then I took Raiden's and Jack's hands in mine. "And these two are my mates, Jack of the North and Raiden, youngest son of Lord Shen of the East."

Orion scanned our party, a calculating look in

his eyes. "You are quite the collector, I see. The next heir to the West, the nephew of the current Northern Lord and all three of the heirs to the east." He chuckled, and his shoulders shook with it. "A bit of a siren, huh?"

My teeth ground as I forced myself not to break the truce already. We hadn't even started to discuss Firestar, and I already wanted to knock this guy's teeth in.

"What can I say?" I smiled sweetly. "I'm truly blessed."

"I bet." The unaligned leader's eyes trailed over me for a moment but not in a lecherous way. Lucky for him, since I could feel the burning hint of power in the palm of my hand just itching to be let loose.

Aeis stepped forward drawing Orion's attention and his son's to her. "I apologize if I'm out of line, but can we see Firestar?" Blake's eyes stayed on Aeis a bit longer than I liked, though she didn't seem bothered by it.

Orion's brows furrowed, and he stroked his jaw. "No apologies needed, but I was under the impression that the fire dragon belonged to your sister here." He pointed a finger in my direction.

Aeis pressed her lips into a thin line and nodded. "Of course, but as you have said yourself, we have traveled a long way, and my sister isn't in any position to be standing out in the elements like this for long periods of time. I just hoped you would want to make her as comfortable as you would your own wife or daughter?" Aeis raised a brow, her soft voice countering the condescending words.

Blake blinked. Five minutes. Five minutes was all it took for my sister to win that man over. If his father didn't think my sister had some sense in her head, then I knew the son did. He'd want to give her whatever she desired just to keep near her.

Thank God for that.

Nodding, Orion turned his gaze back to me. "Your sister is correct. I would be a terrible host indeed and example of the unaligned people if we kept a pregnant woman waiting out here while her mate is held captive inside."

His words made our party relax slightly, but then he waved a finger in the air. "Except," he added, "we are not the ones holding him." He pressed that same finger to his lips in thought. "You have to understand, we accept dragons from all over Waesigar no matter their crimes. Of course, we keep those who might be truly dangerous away from our women and children, but we have to make certain compromises to ensure their safety. That mainly involves us not getting involved in their affairs."

I scoffed. "You're no leader then, if you can't even regulate your own people."

"Maya," Aeis warned, but I shook my head.

"No, I won't hold my tongue any longer." I stepped forward until I was inches from Orion, my eyes firmly on his dark gaze. "I have tried to be civil about this and all you've done is waste our time while the people who have my mate could be killing him right now. I asked nicely for Firestar back, but you're telling me you can't help me. Now, my question to you, Orion, leader of nobody, is why you even bothered with this meeting?" I paused and waited for him to answer, but when he opened his mouth, I added, "Think wisely before you answer, my patience is wearing thin."

I no longer held back the heat in my hand, causing the flame to fill it. I allowed my other hand to crackle with electricity, causing Orion and his men's eyes to lock onto them. They stiffened, and some even drew their weapons, but Orion held a hand up to hold them back.

"Now, I am the one confused, aren't you an earth dragon?" There was some curiosity in his eyes but also fear.

I lifted my hands up, and my eyes slid over to the fire and then the electricity. A slow, wicked grin curled over my face as I said, "Why yes, I am."

"Then how are you …?" he started but was cut off as one of his men decided that they weren't going to wait any longer.

With a yell, he charged at me their sword drawn, wings of ice sprouting from his back.

Traitor. The thought was followed by my hand flying up. The fire shot out, hurtling through the air and hitting him in the chest. It threw him back a few hundred yards behind the group.

It was like someone flipped a switch. The moment I knocked the guy out, the rest of the men around Orion rushed me.

Almost without even thinking about it, the powers came out of me. Vines burst from the ground wrapping around three of them, holding them in place. The electricity in my other hand zapped the closest one to me, the man wiggling on the ground as he convulsed.

Two came at me from either side, and I stomped my foot. The dirt and grass froze, sharp shards of ice bursting upward to chase after them. They weren't quick enough to get away. The ice swept up their legs and over their arms, freezing them in place.

I had never moved so fast in my life. Before I was pregnant, I had been pretty fast on my feet, but now, it was like the others were moving in slow motion, and I could anticipate what they were going to do next. Jack and Raiden had tried to push me behind them and block the attacks, but I was too fast.

By the time they got to me, the only unaligned dragons left standing were Orion and Blake. Orion had a restraining hand on Blake's shoulder, keeping him from coming after me. His own eyes were wide with fear and admiration. Now, that was something I could get used to.

The clearing was quiet for a moment. I relaxed my arms and took in the damage I had done. It'd been a while since I'd been in a fight, and I had to say that even I was impressed. I wasn't even winded.

"Holy crap, Maya," Aeis murmured, her eyes wide. "When did you become such a badass?"

I clicked my tongue and smirked. "What do you think I've been doing cooped up in my room all day? Playing cards?" Raiden and the twins chuckled, but Jack simply stared at me. "What?" I cocked my head to the side. "It's not me. It's your kids who are the badasses." I gestured to my stomach with a grin.

The sound of Orion's throat clearing drew my attention back to him and his son. "I think we got off on the wrong foot," Orion stuttered and then cleared his throat again.

Licking my lips, I offered them a fanged grin. "Now, that's more like it."

13

Orion and Blake led us into the heart of the unaligned camp. Similar to Firestar's when he was working against his father, this settlement had a homier feeling to it.

It was probably because of the children running around and the mothers chastising them to behave. A little girl with auburn hair tied in pigtails not more than six stopped playing with her doll the moment she saw us. She ran in our direction and pointed a finger at my stomach.

"Why are you so fat?"

My mouth dropped open as Aeis giggled. Snapping my mouth closed, I glared at my sister before turning to the little girl. With a soft voice, I explained, "I'm pregnant, not fat."

"So, you have babies in there?" the little girl tilted her head to the side, her nose wrinkling so her freckles stood out more.

"Yes, three of them." I smiled as her eyes widened.

"How'd they get in there?"

The question was so innocent it'd have been cute, had I not been sideswiped by it. I felt like a gaping fish as my mouth opened and closed. I didn't want to lie to the girl, but I wasn't sure it was my place to tell her about the birds and the bees. I glanced back to Jack and Raiden, begging them to help me out with my eyes.

Jack crossed his arms over his chest and turned to ask Orion, "Do the children usually have such freedom around the camp?"

Orion grinned hesitantly. "We try not to let them run too wild, but as long as they don't get past the eastern tent, they're fine."

"What's near the eastern tent?" I asked, happy not to have to answer the little girl but it was her who answered.

She cupped her mouth and leaned in as she whispered, "That's where the naughty people go."

I knelt to her eye level and put my hand over my mouth like her. "Who are the naughty people?"

She started to answer but then glanced toward Orion and clammed up. Instead, she said, "If you want to get a husband, you shouldn't eat so much, or no one will want you. At least, that's what my gran says to my aunt."

Aeis snort-laughed beside me.

That was it. No more Mrs. Nice Guy.

Keeping my voice low, I met the girl's eyes. "I'll have to keep that in mind the next time I eat a baby. The three I have now are giving me a real tummy ache."

The girl gasped, her eyes round as saucers, and then she ran away to some lady sitting by a fire with other women. The woman glanced my way with a mean look that would have Lady Nariko jumping in her skin.

"What'd you say to her?" Aeis asked as Orion led us toward his tent.

"Nothing," I replied, not wanting to hear another lecture, "but my kid won't be anything like that one."

Aeis giggled. "That's what all parents say. Just watch. She'll be like that and more, especially if she's anything like her fathers."

I glanced toward my guys, trailing after Orion and Blake. The thought of a cute little white-headed or dark-haired girl running around made me smile. Even a redhead like the little girl would be fine. As long as they looked like them and not like my late uncle Albert who had a hooked nose and a birthmark that covered the majority of his face. Not that I wouldn't love my kids no matter what they came out to look like, I just wasn't naive enough not to think that a pretty face would make their lives a hell of a lot easier.

"I'm going to have my hands full, aren't I?" I sighed and tugged on the edge of my braid. We stopped outside of a tent that wasn't any larger than the others but had purple flags waving from the door poles.

"Oh, you bet you are, and I'll look forward to spoiling the crap out of those kids too." She winked and darted inside before I could argue.

I started to go in after her, but something caught my eye. In slow motion, I turned my head completely toward what I'd thought I'd seen. A pale head of hair and a glacial set of eyes pinned me in place.

"What is she doing here?" I growled and then turned on Jack who had waited with Raiden for me to go inside.

His eyes followed where I pointed and then narrowed. "I don't know. Nor do I care. She is not my concern nor yours."

"She is, if she's the reason Firestar got kidnapped." I reminded him why we were here. "What if she's the one who told them to take him? No one else knew he was leaving but those in the North."

Jack shook his head. "She was already exiled when Firestar decided to leave."

"How do you know that?" Raiden asked, his biceps bulging as he crossed his arms over his chest. "If you cast her aside, you shouldn't know anything about her whereabouts."

Jack shifted uncomfortably before answering. "I've had someone watching her." When I raised my brows at him, he quickly added, "I just wanted to be sure she left and wasn't planning something. I wanted to keep you safe."

I took a deep breath and let it out, forcing myself to calm down. Jack was only trying to protect me. I would do the same. He couldn't know that the vindictive bitch wouldn't come after us in other ways.

Placing my hands on Jack's arms, I met his

worried gaze. "I believe you. But believe me when I say, there's no way it's a coincidence that she's here, the same place that Firestar was taken to."

"I agree." Jack nodded.

"Me too. The bitch had to be behind this." Raiden dropped his arms and opened the tent flap for us. "Now, how do we prove it?"

Frowning, I walked into the tent and took a seat next to the twins. My sister sat on the other side of them with Orion and Blake at the head of the room. Jack and Raiden took the spots beside me as we waited for Orion to start.

"I apologize for the way we treated you before." Orion ducked his head, genuinely ashamed of his actions. "I simply thought you were some lesser dragon nobles trying to flaunt their status into getting what they wanted. I had no idea you would have such power."

I shifted in my seat at the way he watched me. I didn't like the direction his mind was going in or the way he said power. This had been exactly the thing I wanted to avoid.

"Why is Gretchen here?" I asked, attempting to change the subject from me. When he looked at me in confusion, I elaborated, "The woman out there, white hair, unpleasant in the way that she tried to kill me."

Still, Orion's brows furrowed until his son leaned over and whispered something in his ear. "My son knows the woman you speak of, though I haven't met her myself. As I said before, we accept all kinds of outcasts, no matter their deeds. This woman has committed no crime to our knowledge, so we didn't command her to stay with the others."

"How do you know if someone has committed a crime or not?" Raiden asked, leaning forward with his hands folded in front of him. "They could just lie."

Orion gave a secret smile, a twinkle in his eyes. "We have our spies as do all the regions."

"Well, to be frank," I smirked. "Your spies suck."

The leader tensed but then inclined his head. "Your honesty is refreshing and appreciated. I will make sure to let our operatives know your opinion of their … skills."

"You do that." I narrowed my eyes at him, feeling the threat in his words.

Jack placed his hand on my thigh, not squeezing but just sitting it there. To Orion, he said, "We had a falling out with Gretchen a while ago, but our highest concern is that she might have had a part in Firestar's capture."

"How so?" Orion raised a brow.

"I know for a fact that she still has family in the North. Some of them might have mentioned Firestar's intentions, which she may, in turn, have passed on to some of our other enemies." Jack's grip tightened on my leg and then let go, moving back to his own lap.

"Well, the leak in your own village, I can't help you with but this Gretchen," - Orion exchanged a look with his son - "I can help with that."

Suddenly, Blake stood, his eyes settling on Aeis for a moment before he left the tent. Not more than a moment later, he returned, taking his seat beside Orion like nothing had happened. I started to ask what was going on when a shout jerked my head toward the tent entrance. A few seconds later, Gretchen was dragged in by two burly guards.

"What is the meaning of this? I've done nothing wrong." Gretchen's eyes landed on me, and her struggles strengthened. "You bitch! This is all your fault. You already have my man, you can't just leave me in peace?"

I snorted. "Like I care enough about you to hunt you down. You're the one who can't leave me alone."

Gretchen spit at me. Thankfully, it landed at my feet and not on me. Just the sight of it made my stomach roll.

"Enough." Orion's voice boomed through the tent, cutting off whatever curse Gretchen was going to scream at me. "We let you into our camp, and you bring trouble with you?"

"They're lying. Whatever they're saying about me, it's not true." She pulled until her arms stretched, snarling like a rabid dog.

"So, you didn't tell the men holding their man where they could find him?" Orion arched a brow, and then he turned his head to his son.

Blake sat up straighter. "You were seen several times going past the east tent, into the restricted area."

"There you have it." Orion clapped his hands together and shrugged. "Or would you like these eyewitnesses to be brought forth?" I made a rude noise, making Orion grin. "Our guests don't seem to be in a particularly patient mood. I don't think making them wait any longer will help your cause."

Gretchen let out a low growl before hanging her head. "I might have found out in passing about the fire dragon's movements. And I might have passed it along to some of his fellow fire dragons." She grinned wickedly, and the urge to punch her was strong.

"I've heard enough." Orion nodded toward the guards. "Make sure she is moved to the restricted section." Gretchen gasped and protested, but Orion's eyes were hard. "If you are going to deal with the murderers and thieves, then you can live with them."

Just as he announced her fate, a young blonde woman came rushing through the tent. "Father!" she screamed, her eyes darted around the tent and then landed on Gretchen. "What the hell do you think you're doing?"

"Now, Ellie," Orion held a hand up, trying to soothe the rampaging woman. "You know the rules of our camp. Gretchen has had the same chance as every other member of our camp, and she has broken those rules."

Ellie didn't seem to care about her father's words or anything that was going on. She stomped over to Gretchen and muttered something to her that made the ex-bitch relax in the guards' arms. Ellie then turned and glared at her father.

"I can't believe you. You know what Gretchen has gone through. How can you expect her to change if you punish her at the first sign of weakness?"

I'd have interrupted her, telling her exactly what kind of punishment I thought Gretchen deserved but Ellie was on a roll and wasn't about to let anyone get a word in edgewise.

"Secondly, didn't I tell you I would vouch for her?"

"But you didn't control her like you swore you would," Orion reminded Ellie with a chastising frown.

"You can't control people." Ellie growled, her eyes flashing in anger. "You know that as well as anyone."

I felt like I was missing something in this conversation. Something had happened between these two, and I was curious to know but not rude enough to ask.

"Fine," Orion finally relented. "But this is her last chance." He held his finger up and then looked to Gretchen. "If you break our trust again, I will not hesitate to throw you out. Regardless of what my daughter says." To us, he said, "Come, I will take you to where your man is being held, and I will assure you he will be given back to you."

I sniffed but didn't say what I really thought.

We filed out of the tent and through the village. The little girl from earlier was back to playing with her dolls, my words long forgotten. Her mother, on the other hand, hadn't and shot me a glare as we passed. Soon, we reached the eastern side of the village a large red tent one even bigger than Orion's.

Orion didn't stop but breezed past the tent, a determined pace to his strides. I laced fingers with Raiden and Jack, my heart beating hard in my chest. I'd finally get to see Firestar again. We'd finally be back together again and without any bloodshed.

Well, I smiled to myself, not our own blood anyway.

Stopping in the middle of a clearing, a fire billowing nearby, Orion called out, "Blorder! Get out here!"

The restricted section was a quieter version of the village, with no children playing or women sitting nearby with a watchful eye. There were men of all kinds and manners sharpening weapons, their eyes on us just as keen as any mother's on her children, but with far less noble intentions.

A large man with a bald head came out of one of the tents. The familiar face made my blood boil, and my hand burned with the need to attack. Blorder had been one of Firestar's best men back before we got back together. Then he found out what I could do, and all bets were off. Bye-bye brotherhood and all that shtick. It was not hard to figure how he ended up here, or the fact that he was the one with Firestar.

"Orion," Blorder answered, nodding in respect. Then his eyes landed on my men and me, and that look of respect changed to disgust. "You!"

I couldn't help the smug grin on my lips. "Good to see you too."

His eyes went to my swollen stomach, and the grimace on his face increased. "I see you got what you wanted."

"Yeah." I placed my hand on my stomach, my grin never faltering for a moment. "I guess I did." I tapped my finger on my chin. "Except I'm still missing something, and I think you" - I pointed my finger at him - "are the one who has it, now don't you?"

His eye twitched, but he didn't confirm or deny

it. Instead, he turned his attention to Orion. "Is this how we are to be treated? It's bad enough that you make us stay out here away from the rest of the village, but now we are to be accused of such treacheries?"

"Knock it off," Orion snapped, glancing back at me and then back to Blorder. "This woman believes you have her mate, Firestar. Do you?"

Blorder opened his mouth, and I knew he was going to deny it.

Orion seemed to as well because he added, "If you lie to me, you and your men will be chased out, and then where will you go?"

Growling and stomping his foot, Blorder then snapped his fingers. Another man came forward. "Bring him."

I waited, my hands sweating and my pulse racing. I tried to seem calm on the outside, but inside, I was freaking out, wanting for nothing more than to see Firestar and afraid that it was all a trick.

When they brought him out, I was done holding back. His face was beaten and bloodied, his eye so swollen that it distorted his features. Firestar stumbled forward, barely conscious enough to move, let alone walk. The men holding him tossed him to the ground before us, and I rushed forward, pulling his head into my lap.

"Firestar," I murmured, urging him to look at me. "It's me. I found you."

"Maya," he croaked, his hand reaching up weakly. Before he could get another word out, he had a coughing fit, blood trickling from his mouth.

"What did you do to him?" I growled, glaring up at Blorder.

"Only what he deserved." His eyes filled with glee and I couldn't hold it back any longer. He had to die.

This time, it started from my chest, the icy numbness. It spread across my chest the more I stared at him. My gaze turned cold, and I reached my hand out toward him. Before I could touch him, Orion grabbed my wrist. I turned my eyes on him, accusation written all over my face.

"You can't kill him," Orion told me, not taking his hand off mine.

"He took Firestar," I reminded him, glancing down to where Firestar lay in my arms. "He could have killed him, and this is not the first time. He deserves to die."

"He might." Orion nodded. "But not here, not

in my camp. He is under my protection, and I cannot have you killing him."

I stared up at him, a curse on my tongue. Before I could argue further, a commotion sounded in the distance, followed by footsteps pounding through the woods. Fire dragons burst through the trees, and Lord Amun stood at the front of them.

The cavalry had arrived.

14

Lord Amun was just as large and intimating as his son. At least, to most. To me, he was an angel sent down from heaven, and based on the rage on the lord of the South's face, an avenging angel.

Amun's soldiers burst through the trees that lined the camp, tan colored armor encasing them, swords and fire in their hands. They charged at the outcasts who had been hanging around outside of their tents. They barely had time to grab their own weapons before Amun's men surrounded them. A man to my left threw a fireball at one of the soldiers near him. The soldier dodged it before unleashing one of his own, lighting the guy up.

There were various kinds of dragons, none

more than the other, but all of them just as ready to fight at the sign of a royal army. Several other men were stupid enough to try their luck with the armored soldiers, but soon found themselves flat on their backs. They were lucky that was all they were doing. For what they did to Firestar, I'd have made sure it hurt a hell of a lot more.

Unfortunately for the unaligned men, they were outnumbered and outpowered. Lord Amun's men had them surrounded and incapacitated before you could say jerk chicken. I was more than thankful for their arrival. I might have kicked ass before, but with Firestar in my arms now, I feared that if I started killing, I wouldn't stop.

"Orion!" Lord Amun's voice boomed through the clearing as he stalked across the camp, his wings still burning behind him. "I have let your people trespass on our lands, and this is how you repay me? You house those who would do my son harm?"

I wished I had that kind of presence, to be able to put fear in the eyes of my enemies just from the sound of my voice. The only thing I was able to do on that massive scale was clear a room from eating too many burrito supremes. Bianca and Ryan could attest to that.

Orion didn't freeze in place like the other men,

but he did lose a bit of his commanding aura. It seemed like the unaligned leader wasn't as confident in his position of power as he wanted us to believe. His son started forward as if he were going to defend his father, but Orion waved him off.

"Now, hold a moment, Amun." Orion stepped forward, his hands up in front of him. "We have no knowledge of your son being taken until his mate contacted us." He gestured back toward where I sat with Firestar still clutched in my arms. "As you can see, we have returned your son and were in the process of punishing those who broke our laws."

"What laws?" Blorder growled, crossing his arms over his chest. "The only rules you gave us were to stay on our side of the woods. Other than that, we could do as we wish."

Orion glowered at Blorder, making him snap his mouth shut tight. He then turned back to Lord Amun. "We do our best to give everyone the freedom to rule themselves. Isn't that the reason they come here to begin with?"

"You don't punish those who commit treason?" Lord Amun snarled, his eyes locking onto Blorder who shrank back.

"Technically, it's not treason here." Even Orion knew that was the wrong thing to say, because he quickly tried to add, "But we were in the process of taking care of it."

"No, you weren't," I snapped, shooting dagger at him with my eyes. "You were going to let them go with a hand slap."

Lord Amun looked from me to Orion a frown on his lips. "Is this true?"

Shoulders hunched, Orion started to fumble for a response, but then he seemed to think better of himself. His shoulders straightened, and he stared down Lord Amun. "This is our camp, not yours. We will decide how we punish our citizens."

Stomping toward us, Lord Amun stopped before Orion and Blorder, who at least had the decency to try to shrink into himself. "You forget yourself, Orion. These people are not yours. You may call yourself the unaligned, but as long as you live in Waesigar, you belong to someone. And these men," - he jerked a finger toward Blorder, who paled and stiffened - "have committed treason not only for deserting their posts, but for the capture and torture of their future lord, for which the punishment is death." His eyes were hot as molten lava as he stared down the quaking ex-guard.

I wanted to stand up and cheer. If I had some pom-poms, I would have shaken them for all they were worth. I'd always liked Lord Amun. He wasn't so much of a hothead like his son, probably because of his age, but when he did lose it, it was for good reason.

This was a very good reason.

Blorder stared at his ex-lord and sovereign and then turned his gaze to Orion. When Orion didn't immediately stand up for him, Blorder lost his confidence. Falling to his knees in front of Lord Amun, Blorder begged like the worm he was.

"Please, my lord! We were only thinking of our people. Your son withheld something from us that would have made us more powerful than all of the other regions. Do you not think that too deserves to be punished?" Blorder waited before Lord Amun, his shoulders shaking but his gaze firm.

Lord Amun glared down at Blorder for a moment and then crossed his arms over his chest. "What is this thing that he has withheld? That you think is worth dying for?"

Before Blorder could open his mouth to answer, I beat him to it. "Me." Lord Amun's head snapped to me. "Firestar was protecting me from his men. The men who wanted to rape me for my powers or more precisely the powers I could give them."

Just the thought of it made me sick to my stomach. Sure, Lady Nariko had offered to pay me for my services, but Blorder and his men wanted to take me. I had no doubt that they would have enjoyed every second of it, and the moment I wasn't of any use to them, they would have killed me. Or worse.

Staring down at me, his brow furrowed, Lord Amun seemed horrified and curious by my words. "I'm not sure I follow you."

"Let me explain then." Jack pushed his way forward until he stood at my back, his shins pressing against me. "Lady Maya can increase the powers of those she mates with." He held his hand out in front of him, ice building up in his palm, lengthening and shaping into the form of his warhammer.

I sat still as a statue as I watched Lord Amun and Orion's reactions. We were taking a chance by telling them what we could really do. So far, we had kept it under wraps, with only rumors of what I could do circulating the regions. To finally set the record straight could help us … or bite us in the ass.

"That's remarkable." Orion's eyes widened as he stared down at Jack's hammer. "And to think your men have as much power as you." He shook his head and wiped a hand over his face. "I greatly apologize. You could have decimated us if you wanted to, and you didn't."

The fact that Orion didn't even mention the fact that I could give him or his own son powers added points to his scorecard. Ones that he needed desperately if he expected me to forgive and forget his other transgressions.

Now, there was only Lord Amun to worry about. I blinked up at him, worried about what I would find on his face. Would he be afraid? In awe like Orion? Or greedy like Lady Nariko?

The thoughtful look on his face made me nervous. What was he thinking?

"And does my son have this power as well?" His gaze softened and settled on Firestar who had passed out. I nodded. Lord Amun glanced behind me to Raiden. "And you too?"

Raiden didn't hesitate to whip his trident out, spinning it in the air like the show-off he was. He struck a cocky pose with a grin on his face. I shook my head, unable to hold back the grin even in our grim situation.

"Well," Lord Amun huffed, "it's obvious what has happened here. Lady Maya and the others are true mates. Which means ..." His gaze turned hard again as it landed on Blorder. "That taking her by force would have been a complete waste of time, as well as a death sentence for you and your men."

I let out a shaky breath, my pulse slowing. Thank God. I had feared Lord Amun would have agreed with Blorder and that I would have to hurt my father-in-law. I didn't know if what he said was true. All I knew about my abilities was that I did the deed with them, and they got powers. Why it happened now and not when I had mated with Firestar the first time I couldn't even begin to guess. Maybe I hadn't been old enough? Who knew?

All that mattered was that Lord Amun saw what really was going on, and Blorder would get what was coming to him. Him and his band of power-hungry men.

"Now." Lord Amun tugged on the belt of his pants and then waved a few of his soldiers who surrounded the area forward. "If you would be so kind as to surrender my men over to me, I would be glad to escort them back to their families before they are tried and punished. I will also be taking my son, his mate, and the rest of her company with us as well." He paused and placed his hands on his hips, a brow raised. "Unless you have a problem with that?"

Orion shook his head and waved a hand. "No,

no. Please take them. I'm not looking to pick a fight." He then turned his tired and worn face to me. "I can't apologize enough, Lady Maya. Please, if you need anything in the future, do not hesitate to call on us."

I inclined my head. I might just have to take him up on that offer … after I took care of Firestar.

Several of Lord Amun's men came forward and knelt beside me. I allowed them to take Firestar from my arms and lay him on a makeshift stretcher. As they carried him out of the camp and into the trees they had burst through not long before, I found Jack and Raiden. Leaning back into them, I sighed.

"Will he be okay?" My words were so soft I almost didn't think they heard me.

"The damage didn't look too bad. I'm sure he will be fine," Raiden murmured in my ear, his hand squeezing my shoulder in reassurance.

I had a hard time believing him only because I had seen how much pain Firestar had been in. It didn't help that all around us, the men of Blorder's camp were dragged out of their tents and forced into the trees. There were less of them than the first time I'd been threatened by them. It seemed Blorder had lost some of his supporters when he left the south. A blessing but still, I wouldn't feel safe until they were judged.

"Let's be on our way," Jack announced, offering me his arm. "We might have won this battle, but we still have a war to fight and a kingdom to rescue."

I took his arm with a grim smile. "Yeah, I'm ready to go." I glanced over my shoulder to tell Aeis to come on, the twins having followed Firestar out, but she was in deep discussion with Blake. She threw her head back and laughed as Blake gave her a lecherous grin.

Geez, Louise. I rolled my eyes.

"Aeis!" I shouted, making her clam up. "Stop your flirting, we're leaving."

She sent me a death stare that only a sibling could give you before saying something to Blake. He nodded and brushed a hand across her cheek, making her face redden. Aeis walked toward us, a bit of a sway to her step.

I coughed to cover up the laugh at her obvious display.

"What?" Aeis asked with a raised brow.

"Nothing." I grinned and then coughed, "Harlot."

"What was that?" Aeis's eyes narrowed into slits, and I grinned.

"I didn't say anything. You must be hearing things." I pushed forward with Jack and Raiden, leaving my sister's suspicious glare burning into my back.

Once we had left the camp and made our way into the trees, we could breathe freely again. We had gotten Firestar back, had fewer enemies out to get us, and Lord Amun's men to help us in the fight to come. Overall, I didn't think we came out of it too badly.

Lord Amun waited for us just on the edge of the woods, his eyes on the soldiers assigned to hold Blorder and his men. When we approached him, he turned that watchful gaze our way. I forced myself not to wilt against the heavy weight of his eyes. Though, after the last hour, I was more than ready to collapse into bed.

"I was unaware that you had more than one mate," were the first words to come out of Lord Amun's mouth.

I winced at finally being caught and then wished I could take it back. I was far from being ashamed of having more than one mate, and it was time to fess up to all our lies. How else would we expect Lord Amun and his men to help us?

"Lord Amun, I admit Firestar and I had misled

you before." I stepped away from Jack and Raiden, needing to do this on my own. "The truth is I am mated to all three of them, and I love them each equally."

"I thought as much." He shifted and then nodded toward my stomach. "And the child? Who does that belong to?"

My lips spread out into a wide smile as my hand curved over my belly. "All of them." Lord Amun raised a curious brow. "I'm having triplets."

This time, Lord Amun laughed. Head thrown back, belly shaking laughter. I chanced a peek at Raiden and Jack who only shrugged. When I turned back to Lord Amun, he wiped his eyes with the pad of his thumb.

"You, girl, are something else. If I didn't know your father, I'd wonder if you were crazy."

I didn't know if I should be offended or not. So instead of saying anything, I said nothing at all.

Lord Amun sighed and stared back at his men gathering to leave. "Should I assume the promise to pay my debt is also a falsehood?"

"No!" I answered louder than I meant to. I cleared my throat and tried again. "I mean, no. It was not my intention to lie about that. I do plan to pay your debts. After all, we can't have the South being taken over by some loan shark."

"Loan shark?" Lord Amun chuckled. "That's a funny way to describe Drac. He's more of a pirate, but not any less dangerous."

Raiden and Jack exchanged a look before turning to me, but I was way ahead of them. Taking a step closer to Lord Amun, I asked, "How would you like to wipe that debt out altogether?"

15

Lord Amun and his men set up camp a bit further into the southern region. The camp wasn't much different than that of the unaligned, except we had a lot more armored dragons patrolling the area.

"How can he afford this if he has been sending all his money to Drac?" I asked Jack over dinner, which consisted of some meat broth stew that'd been cooked over the fire. The babies didn't really care for it, but I was so hungry that I ignored them for once, forcing it down.

"I can imagine Lord Amun stopped paying him the moment you promised to help him, which probably didn't make Drac very happy." Jack paused, a thoughtful expression on his face. "I wonder if that was around the time that Lady Nariko called on his services? Perhaps that is why Lord Amun has not seen any retribution for his actions."

"Drac is pulling all his resources to help Lady Nariko keep the East," I mused aloud, dipping my spoon back into my bowl. "He probably can't be bothered with an unpaid loan right now."

"Which is what will bite him in the ass," Raiden added with a grin and a wink.

I grinned in return as I stuck the spoon in my mouth. I rolled the meat around, savoring the juice like it was going to be my last meal for a long time. For all I knew, it might be.

After I told Lord Amun of our plans to take back the East and who currently held the border, he was more than happy to supply his men to the cause. Now, we had men from the North, my father's whole army from the West, and the Southern army. If that wasn't enough to take the kingdom back, then I didn't know what would.

"When are we going to make our move?" I swallowed the bit in my mouth. "We can't wait too much longer. I'm sure they have spies just like Orion does. They must know what we are up to."

"Oh, I'm sure they do," Raijin answered, taking a seat across from us by the fire. "If I know my mother, which I do, then she will have already found out we have the backing of the North and West."

"Hopefully, she doesn't know about the South yet," Fujin added, sitting down next to his brother. "We can get the jump on them if they think they outnumber us."

I frowned my brow furrowed. "How many men does Drac have?"

"Thousands," Fujin answered, picking up a bowl from the ground. He took a bite of the stew but didn't make a face like I had. Guess it was just me.

"And we have?" I glanced around the camp, calculating how many men I saw and how many were waiting back up north.

"Well, we have the few hundred from the North." Jack started, tapping his spoon on the side of his bowl.

"We do have a few hundred still on the inside," Raijin contributed and then glanced around as well. "I'd say Lord Amun has about five hundred or so. Not enough to take on Drac, or he'd have done it before."

I nodded my agreement. "My father's army the last time I counted has close to a thousand."

"Two thousand," my sister corrected me, stepping around the twins to take a seat between them. I stared at her, unsure of her count. She raised a brow and smirked. "You've been gone a long time, and we haven't had a war in a while. What can I say?" Aeis shrugged. "Our father likes to be prepared."

"Amen for that." Fujin grinned at her, bumping his shoulder against hers. She smiled shyly in return. I'd bet my left foot something was going on there. Maybe not to the mating stage but definitely something.

"So, we have about as many as he does, if not more." I stared down into my bowl, not really seeing it as my mind whirled. "Have we sent word to your men yet?" I asked my sister, glancing up from my bowl.

Nodding, she accepted her bowl from Raijin. "As soon as we made camp, I sent word. They should be on their way along with the Northern men as well. I told them to stay on their side of the border and out of sight. No need to give them the advantage of seeing our hand."

"Good call," Raiden said. He reached out for my bowl. "Are you done?" I let him take my bowl and help me to my feet. "I figure Firestar is probably waking up soon. We better fill him in before someone else does, and we have to hear about it for the next week."

I giggled and tucked my hair behind my ear. "Not like you wouldn't have done the same."

"At least I didn't get captured," Raiden retorted, leading me away from the others. I let my hand brush over Jack's shoulder as I passed, his fingers coming up to touch mine.

They had put Firestar in a tent next to his father's, one we were supposed to share but weren't while he was healing. We were lucky they had brought a medic along with them when they came, something we had forgotten to do ourselves. Then again, we hadn't expected to have to carry him out.

Guilt ate at me as I remembered how he looked when we first got him back. On the outside, he looked near beaten to death. Why they hadn't gone ahead and finished the job, I didn't know. Maybe they wanted to draw it out, make him really pay. Or maybe they even wanted to use him as bait to get to me. We wouldn't know until Firestar woke up and told us.

Raiden pushed open the flap to the tent and ushered me inside. He didn't follow me though, closing the flap behind me. I appreciated the time alone with Firestar and wondered how Raiden had guessed I wanted it.

He was probably trying to get me to rest some too. I tended to overdo it, especially lately. Though I was three babies deep and couldn't see my toes, I felt like a real superhero. That's when I wasn't looking at the wrong side of the toilet.

"Maya," Firestar's voice pulled me from my thoughts. My eyes trailed over the dirt floor they had covered with a beat-up rug to the cot they'd set up on the far side of the tent. The room was barely lit with a lantern sitting on the wooden table. It was hard to see much of anything but shadows, much less Firestar's condition. I supposed that was the point.

"Hey," I murmured, coming over to him to kneel by the cot.

His face was swollen and bruised from the beating, but he still looked like himself. I had no doubt that a few days from now, he would be in tip-top fighting shape. We healed faster than humans, but we still needed time. Sadly, time wasn't something we had in large supply.

"How are you feeling?" It was a stupid question, but I needed something to talk about besides the impending fight. He didn't need to worry about that, not right now.

Firestar shifted and groaned. "Like I got beaten to hell and back." He huffed and laughed. "I can't believe they got the jump on me."

"Shh, now." I brushed his hair back from his face. "You couldn't have known they were coming. It was that damn Gretchen."

His eyes narrowed at her name. "That's who did this?" Firestar jerked in bed, trying to sit up, but I put my hand on his chest to keep him down. "Please tell me you killed her. That they didn't just cast her aside again." The pure fury in Firestar's eyes was understandable, and I hated to see how he'd react when he found out she was still out there.

Why did I always get stuck with the shit jobs? Damn Raiden. Now, I knew why he left me with him alone. Sneaky bastard.

"I don't know what happened to her. We left her with Orion, the leader of the unaligned." It wasn't a lie. I really didn't know what being sent to the restricted section of the camp meant. We'd taken the majority of those living there. So, maybe she would die of loneliness or spite. One could dream.

"How'd we get out?"

I relaxed, knowing he'd let it go. "Your father

came riding in to the rescue, or rather flying." I frowned, remembering an important question I needed to ask. "So, what did Blorder want from you? Just to get revenge?"

Firestar jerked at his blanket, visibly irritated at just the name of his ex-guard. "The asshole never really said. Some days, it was just to get back at me for dragging them away from their families. Other days, it was because he wanted me to tell him where you were. When I refused, he broke my arm."

My heart ached at his words, and once more, I wished I could be the one to kill the bastard. I'd have to just trust that Lord Amun would take care of him and that justice would prevail. And there was always the option of sneaking in and killing him myself. You know, if it came down to it.

"Hey, one good thing did come out of all this." I smiled at him. "He's even agreed to help us taken down Drac and Lady Nariko. Did you know Drac is the man he owed money to?"

Firestar frowned. "No, I didn't. I knew it was some rich crook, but he never told me who it was."

I stroked his arm and took his hand in mine. "Well, as luck would have it, our enemy is one and the same."

"Well, at least, that's taken care of." Firestar's

hand held mine tightly, his thumb sliding along mine. "I'm assuming he figured out I'm not the only one."

My lips twisted into a grimace. "Yeah, and about the power stuff. Though he took it surprisingly well and even helped deter anyone else from trying to do what Lady Nariko wanted to do."

He hummed but didn't say anything. We sat there in companionable silence, both of us lost in thought, which was fine with me. I'd had enough action for the day. Hell, the week. If I didn't have to fight again anytime soon, that would be great, though it wasn't likely. Not when there were still people out there who wanted to hurt us.

"How are the babies?" His eyes went to my stomach and he shifted on the cot to touch it. I placed my hand over his, moving closer so he wouldn't have to strain so much. "Any new developments?"

"They're fine. Missing their daddy." I grinned at him. "But good."

"And their mother?"

I ducked my head, paying close attention to our hands linked together. "Tired, but that could be because I kicked some major ass in the unaligned camp." I glanced up at him with a smug grin.

"You what?" Firestar's eyes widened, but it wasn't from surprise but concern. "What were you even doing there to begin with, let alone kicking ass?"

Irritation filled me. "I'll have you know that while you were getting kidnapped, I've been practicing. I'm a bad mama jama now. I can take care of myself."

Firestar scoffed and turned his head away before sighing, meeting my eyes once more. "The problem is that you shouldn't have to take care of yourself. What's the point of us all being together as a team if you don't let us do our part?"

"Do your part?"

Firestar grabbed my arm and dragged me down to him, his lips covering mine in a heated kiss. When he was done, he pushed me back, his eyes hot with anger.

"How can we protect you if you don't let us? You aren't the only one who is afraid of losing someone. I'd die a million deaths. Let them torture me. Cut me. If it meant keeping you alive. Our children alive."

My eyes burned, and I swallowed thickly. "I know. I know." I patted his chest, glancing down at the rise and fall of his breathing. "But would it be so bad to let me do the saving every once in a while?"

Firestar chuckled. "I suppose not." His hand caressed my face, and he kissed me again. When he pulled back this time, he didn't let me go. "So, tell me about this ass kicking."

I leaned back on my heels and smiled as I retold what happened before we saved him. The look on Firestar's face was worth every minute of the drama that occurred. The way his eyes widened, and he laughed. The awe and wonder at my newfound control over my powers, there was really nothing like it. I couldn't wait to show him how far I'd come in real life. He'd be so proud of me.

"I'm proud of you," Firestar said as if reading my mind. "You continued your training even after I left, even after you found out I'd gone missing. I'd half expected you to come charging in half-cocked."

My mouth dropped open. "I would do no such thing. I'll have you know I was as cool as a cucumber." Firestar quirked a brow, and I laughed. "Okay, okay. I wasn't. At first, I wanted to chase after you the moment we found out that you were missing. Then Jack and Raiden pretty much gave me the same lecture you did. They need me, and you'd be pissed if they let me get killed."

"Damn straight."

I smirked. "Not that it really helped much."

Firestar's lip drooped. "Then how did they convince you to stay?"

Licking my lips, a wicked grin covered my lips. "Let's just say they had to tag team me."

The look of confusion on his face made me laugh, but I didn't elaborate. He'd figure it out, if Raiden didn't fill him in later. Just imagining that conversation made me grin.

"Anyway, it was even worse when I found out where you were being kept. I wanted to come after you right away. Fuck politics. Fuck having a plan." I waved my hand in front of me to emphasize my point.

"Well, looks like it all worked out." Firestar let out a heavy breath and then winced as he shifted.

"Yeah, besides you getting your ass kicked." I stood and patted Firestar's hand. "I should let you rest. You've been through enough."

Firestar snorted. "Like you haven't?"

I gave a tired smile. "I'll go to bed soon too, but I want to find out when we are going to march on the East before that happens. I'd had my fair share of being left out of meetings to last me a lifetime."

Rolling his eyes, Firestar grunted. "I guess that means I'll be taking your place in the dark."

I snickered. "I'll come and fill you in, promise." I squeezed his hand and backed away slowly. "Though I can't promise it won't be without my own commentary added. Those things can get really boring."

Firestar chuckled. "I can't wait."

16

Four days. It took four days for Firestar to heal and get back on his feet. The rest of our army would be in position by the next day. Everything was almost in position. Soon, it would be over.

"Damn it!" Firestar shouted, batting my hand away as he stood in the middle of our tent. "Not so tight."

I rolled my eyes and continued to lace up Firestar's armor. "Stop being such a baby."

"I'm injured, woman. I can be a baby if I want to," Firestar growled, shooting me a look over his shoulder.

"You're not injured anymore. The medic gave you a clean bill of health just last night. So, don't be trying that bullshit on me." I finished, tightening the last tie before moving around to the front of him. We'd decided to try on his armor before the big day to make sure it fit. We were lucky his father had the foresight to bring Firestar's armor. Otherwise, he'd have to borrow someone else's. I couldn't imagine the drama queen he'd be then.

"Doesn't mean I'm not still sore," Firestar grumbled and shifted uncomfortably.

I straightened his shoulder pad, so it sat better underneath his armor. I had my own set of armor, but I didn't think I would be fitting into that anytime soon. Not that they guys would even think of letting me anywhere near the battle.

I might be a badass with my new powers, but I was still pregnant, and a pregnant woman in battle wasn't a good idea. I'd be a nice distance from the battle, but not so far away I couldn't see how it was going. I'd have about fifty or so soldiers with me as well as Lord Amun keeping me company. We were supposed to take out any stragglers that got away from the fight and tried to escape for the trees.

"Why aren't you giving the other guys the same treatment?" Firestar asked, brushing my hands away to adjust the straps himself.

Crossing my arms under my chest, I shrugged.

"Who said I'm not? You're just the first one on my list because you're the one who needs the most—"

"Pity?"

"Help," I corrected him with a raised brow. "Are you sure you want to be doing this? Like you said, you're still sore. I almost lost you once. I don't want you getting put in danger again if you're not up for it."

"I'm up for it," Firestar snapped, glaring at me for even mentioning it.

Hands up in defense, I backed up a step. "Hey, don't bite my head off for being concerned. You're just as afraid of me getting hurt as I am for you. Or have you forgotten?" I slid a hand over my stomach, daring him to argue.

Firestar sighed and ran a hand through his hair, mussing it. "I'm sorry, I just hate being treated like an invalid."

I snorted. "I know how you feel."

Not bothering to argue with me, Firestar bent down and re-tied his boots for the hundredth time. "I know I scared you, hell everyone, but you have to remember I was in the last war. I've been hurt far worse than what that piece of shit Blorder could do."

As he stood up straight, I stepped closer to him.

I placed my hand on his chest and arched up on my tiptoes until our mouths were brushing each other. "If you get hurt, I will kill you."

Firestar grunted. I nipped at his lower lip, drawing it away from him before letting it go with a pop. "You think I'm kidding, but if you ever scare me like that again …" I reached down, my hand trailing down his chest and across his stomach, then to the front of his pants where his hardened length waited for me. I stroked him twice, long and hard before grabbing hold of him. "I will rip your favorite appendage from your body and serve it to your men on a platter. Do you understand?"

Barking a laugh, Firestar knocked his forehead against mine before his hand covered the one holding his precious bits. "I missed you too."

I released him but not before giving him another tight squeeze, pressing my lips hard against his mouth so our teeth butted. "Don't do anything stupid."

"Yes, ma'am." Firestar's laughter followed me as I left his tent and went to hunt down the other two members of our foursome.

No one paid me much mind as I made my way through the camp. Everyone was too busy either getting ready for the battle or making the most of what could be their last night alive. I hoped that later tonight, I would be one of those people. I finally had all three of my guys back together, and I wanted to make sure I memorized every inch of them before we went into the thick of things.

I found Raiden with his brothers, playing dice with my sister and a few others. From the looks of it, all of them, from the way my sister had her hair undone, and her hand on Raijin's thigh, had already started the drinking.

Coming up behind them, I let my hand trail along the back of Raiden's shoulders. He glanced up from the game, his eyes softening when he saw me. Suddenly, his arm wrapped around my waist and dragged me into his lap.

Giggling, I slapped his chest but snuggled against him. "I see you aren't too worried about the upcoming fight." I splayed my fingertips along the side of his jaw, tracing his lips.

He nipped at my fingers playfully. "Why worry? We outnumber them by more than a thousand. We have three overpowered dragons, thanks to your delicious pu—"

I slapped a hand over his mouth as his eyes lowered to my lap. Chuckling behind my hand, his tongue darted out to lick my palm.

I pulled it away with a giggle and a grimace. "Ew. I can't believe you did that."

His chest rumbled as he laughed even harder. His voice lowered as he bumped his head against the side of mine, his breath hot in my ear. "I've been in every part of you, and you're worried about my spit on your hand?"

"I could think of a few places that might need a reminder." I gave him a heated look, licking my lips in what I hoped was a seductive manner.

"Alright, guys, I'm out." Raiden suddenly announced, standing with me still in his arms. I squeaked and grabbed the back of his neck, holding on for dear life.

The twins chuckled and Aeis made a face before turning her attention back to whispering in Fujin's ear, her hand on his thigh now as well. I bet I wasn't the only one getting some tonight.

Raiden started away from the group, and I glanced around, noticing we weren't headed toward the tent Firestar was in. "Wait, where are we going?"

Raiden grinned cheekily. "You'll see." He headed out of the camp and toward the woods. When he kept walking for a few minutes, I pushed at his embrace.

"If we're going to be going much further, I'd rather walk, thanks." To my relief, Raiden let me down. When my feet the ground, I searched around us once more. "Wait a moment, isn't this …?"

Raiden didn't answer me but just kept up with his secretive smile. The area we were in was familiar. So much so that I started walking without him, moving where my feet knew I should go.

Within a few moments, I heard water. My feet moved faster, and before long I broke the tree line and stood before a waterfall. The exact same one Raiden and I had—

"Do you remember?" Raiden's voice in my ear made me jump and spin around. "This is the first time we …"

I glanced back at the waterfall and then to him. "I didn't think we were this close to our border. How'd you even know?"

His hands grasped my hips and drew me closer. "You think I'd forget something this important?" Raiden's head dipped down, his lips brushing my ear. "Every taste, every touch. The very first time I was inside of you. It's all ingrained in my memory." He spun me around to see Jack and Firestar, who had somehow sneaked up behind us.

The armor I'd worked so hard to fit onto

Firestar had been removed. He stood shirtless, the scars of his recent injury still there. Even though it was dark, I could make out the red of newly-healed skin. My hands itched to touch him, to remind me he was still okay.

Jack stood next to him, his suit jacket discarded, and his dress shirt unbuttoned. The line of skin beneath gleamed beneath the moonlight. He had left his hair undone, and it fluttered in the slight breeze. Just the sight of them together like this was almost too much for me.

"Now, we'll make a new memory." Raiden interrupted my thoughts as he led me forward. "One you will keep close to heart."

I swallowed thickly, my heart pounding in my chest. "Not that I'm complaining, I've dreamed of us all together like this but … why? Why now?"

Jack stepped forward, his hand outstretched to me. I took it letting him bring me near. "Tomorrow, the others will be here. We might not have a chance to have a moment like this for a long time. This battle could draw out for days, weeks even."

"Don't talk like that." I shook my head, my eyes burning. "We outnumber them. It'll be like shooting fish in a bucket."

"You know that's not true." Firestar shifted

closer, his hand on my waist. "We cannot predict what will happen tomorrow any more than we know what will happen in the next few minutes."

Raiden chuckled. "Well, I don't know about you guys, but I plan to see what Maya looks like naked and wet in the moonlight."

Firestar snorted. "Such a romantic."

"Hey, I thought it was," Raiden turned his lust-filled gaze to mine. I held a hand out to him, bringing him closer to me.

"Promise me something," I whispered, though I wasn't sure why. Maybe it was the ambiance or something. "Promise that you'll come back to me. All of you." I looked around at the three of them, my heart in my throat.

Instead of answering me, hands - I didn't know whose - pulled my shirt up and over my head. Another set worked on my pants, and before I knew it, I stood naked in the middle of three overly dressed men.

"Now, that's hardly fair," I started and then my words caught in my throat as fingers stroked my wet slit. They were like a pack of starving wolves the way they fell upon me. Mouths here, hands there, I could only tell who was who if I focused really hard, but they weren't letting me get a chance to do so.

By the time they had me writhing and begging, they had discarded their own clothes. Their contrasting bodies rubbed against every inch of me, none of them fighting for dominance over the other. It almost felt like it was rehearsed.

"Since when—" I breathed, cut off as I let out a sharp gasp as my leg found its way over someone's shoulders, a tongue delving between my thighs. "Did you guys have time to plan this?"

"When you were so busy spying on your sister and the twins," Jack rumbled in my ear. Okay, not the one down under. His cool hand slid down my back and cupped my ass as his mouth found the junction of my neck. He kissed and nibbled there before pulling back. "Tonight, don't think about tomorrow. Or what might happen. Just feel us. Love us. And let us love you."

My head fell back onto his shoulder as the mouth on me brought me to my release. Another mouth latched onto one of my nipples, its owner's hand massaging the other one. My legs quivered and fell out from beneath me, making them have no choice but to hold on to me or let me fall.

Someone's arms wrapped around my waist and the cool night air brushed my folds. My eyes fluttered open to see a redhead move back to help lay me on the ground. Damn Firestar knew how to play me just right.

Now, normally, I'd complain about the ground being cold and uncomfortable, but with three equally delicious men surrounding me, I hardly had a moment to think, let alone care what the ground felt like. Besides, I didn't stay on the ground for long. Raiden pulled me half up into his lap, so my head leaned against his chest as he resumed his fondling of my breasts, pulling the peaks until I gasped in a mixture of pleasure and pain.

Jack leaned down to capture my mouth, our tongues tangling as my legs were spread wide. I wrapped my arms around Raiden's back, holding on to him in my strange position as I readied myself for what was to come. I didn't have to wait long, the head of Firestar's length bumped against my entrance before pushing completely in with one fell swoop.

I cried out against Jack's mouth, his hand moving from cupping my chin to holding me in place. Firestar dragged my legs up higher as he thrust into me at a different angle and I swore, my eyes rolled back into my head. A cool palm caressed my stomach lovingly, touching it before moving lower. Dipping between my legs, a finger pressed against my sensitive nub. My hips bucked just as Firestar withdrew, and this time I had to rip my mouth away from Jack to cry out.

"Fuck!" My back arched as pleasure exploded through my core. Firestar grunted, his hands tightening on my thighs. He stayed there for a moment before moving out from between my legs. Raiden shifted out from behind me, so that he and Firestar could trade places.

I'd barely come down from the peak when Raiden pushed into me. His movements were different than Firestar's more demanding one. He didn't just coax my orgasm from me, he commanded it, which only made it all the sweeter.

My mind was too muddled to even comprehend what was happening as I was shifted around. I'd already been worked up so much by Raiden and Firestar that Jack just eased right in. It didn't take many pumps before I was already on the edge. Each orgasm ended up stronger than the previous, and this one wasn't any different.

Screams ripped from my throat, echoing in the night. If I hadn't been close to passing out, then I'd worry about the rest of the camp hearing us, but I couldn't remember my own name, let alone care if my sister heard my cries of passion.

Completely spent, I collapsed into the arms of Firestar - I thought it was him anyway - I couldn't see anything but the inside of my eyelids at that point. The enemy could attack us at that very moment, and I could have cared less. I could barely focus on breathing, let alone fighting.

"Man," I half laughed, my breathing heavy. "If I'd known I'd get that kind of treatment, I'd say we should go to war more often."

A round of chuckles followed my admission. Hands stroked my skin in calming patterns. No one bothered to move as we caught our breath and soaked in what we'd just done.

"I don't know about you guys, but I don't think I can move." I tried to sit up but gave up halfway. "Nope, not gonna happen."

Raiden laughed and stroked my hair away from my face. "Are you in a hurry?"

I shook my head or tried to. It ended up being the barest of movements.

"Not to be the bearer of bad news," Jack said with a level voice. How was that even possible? He should be as shaken as me. Not fair, I tell you. "But we have a big day ahead of us. We should probably get Maya to bed soon."

"Fine." Raiden sighed and stood, his lower lip poking out into a pout.

I laughed and then groaned as everyone shifted from the ground. Firestar still had me in his lap as he stood. He lifted me from the ground, causing me to groan again. I ached everywhere but in the best of ways. In an 'I better get to do that again' kind of way.

Firestar shot me a knowing grin. "Let's go get you cleaned up." Before he headed toward the waterfall. This was going to be cold.

17

The day should have been dreary and gray. That's how all wars were fought, weren't they? I remembered making the last battle of the *Waesigar* video game raining and dark. As if that would make the fight more dramatic. Harder.

It didn't though. The ominous setting only made those fighting grumpy and disheartened. Not that the sun beaming down on us now made me any happier.

"Isn't it supposed to be raining or something?" Raiden asked, staring up at the sky as if he read my mind.

It was scary how the guys seemed so in tune

with my thoughts and feelings lately. Probably a combination of our close relationship and the babies inside of me. I could only imagine what it would be like when I was further along. The same went for my powers. If they kept increasing over my pregnancy, I might have a problem just leaving the house, let alone being able to walk without waddling.

"I know what you mean," Jack added, pulling me from my thoughts. He adjusted the ties on his armor and tilted his face up. "If I close my eyes, I could almost pretend like we are out on a picnic."

Firestar snorted. "If you can get past the smell of dirty men and sulfur." His nostrils flared to prove his point.

He had a good one. It was hard to pretend that we weren't going off to battle. There were too many of us in too small of an area.

People liked to think that war was a big, magnificent thing. Hair streaming through the air as they sliced their swords into their enemies, blood spraying in perfect arcs as they painted the ground around them. But really, most of it was disgusting, with people pissing wherever they felt like it. Bathing was rare, though we were close enough to a small river to take care of that bit.

I doubted Drac and his men were completely in the dark about what we were doing. Just a single uptake of wind, of which there had been many, and our collective stench would alert the enemy to our presence. I could only hope our numbers would outweigh our lack of a surprise attack.

"Well," I started, hoping to lessen the tension we were all feeling, "maybe we'll end the fight fast enough, we can have a picnic." I gave them a small smile which they didn't return. A series of stares turned on me, and I shrugged. "What?"

Raiden chuckled and shook his head, wrapping an arm around my shoulders. "Sure, Maya. We'll have a picnic right on top of the corpses. That'll be romantic."

I shoved at his chest. "It's not funny. I'm just trying to make everything not so …" I waved my hand in the air.

"Morbid?" Jack leaned in to answer, a hint of a smile on his lips.

Nodding, my throat thick with emotion, I replied, "Yeah, that."

Jack caressed the side of my face, warmth in his pale eyes. "Don't get too caught up in what might happen. It'll distract you from what is to come."

Letting out a heavy breath, I nodded again.

Turning away from him slightly, I scanned the area around us. No one was really paying much attention to us, they were too absorbed in their preparations. I hadn't seen my sister or the twins yet. Part of me didn't want to know where they were, especially if they were doing naughty things.

Don't get me wrong. I was happy for her. She needed some fun in her life. After all the sadness and rejection, Aeis deserved happiness.

As if knowing I was thinking of her, Aeis appeared with Lord Amun. She spoke quietly with him and then glanced up. Her eyes searched around before landing on me. With a grim expression on her face, she said something else to Lord Amun, who nodded and then looked my way. Leaving the lord, Aeis walked toward me.

She looked like how a warrior dragoness should. Tall, commanding, her eye set with a fierce determination, like she knew what was to come and she couldn't give a shit how big and bad they were. Plus, she looked way better in her armor than I did in mine.

I frowned down at my own ill-fitting set. I couldn't wear my normal suit, not with my belly protruding out like it was. The way the guys told it,

I wouldn't need it anyway because no one was getting past them to where I would be waiting.

"You don't look happy." Aeis stopped before us, her eyes giving the guys a cursory look before settling back on me. "You get to stay out of the fight."

I frowned harder. She said it like I wanted to be stuck here. Like I wanted to watch my mates go off to battle where I couldn't help them. For all the powers the babies have given me, I still couldn't use them to save those I loved. It wasn't fair.

"Don't rub it in." Raiden slung an arm around my shoulders. "Maya's feeling a bit left out right now."

I shrugged his arm off. "No, I'm not." I scowled at Aeis. "Aren't you supposed to be getting ready to lead our men into battle? What are you still doing over here?"

Aeis was supposed to lead our father's army into battle. I didn't know why she had waited this long to go to her position, we'd be starting at any time. We were just waiting for the trumpets to sound.

Aeis shifted in place, a faint blush spreading across her cheeks. "I will be. I was just saying good-bye."

"Good-bye to who?" I asked just as the twins came barreling into the area, laughing and joking with each other. When they saw Aeis, they immediately stopped and beamed at her, causing her to blush even more.

"Come on, dude." I shook my head, my lips twisted in disgust. "I don't need to know. Just go make sure we're not going to lose this thing."

Aeis slid her eyes to the side, a silent exchange between her and Jack that I couldn't figure out. As soon as it happened, it was over, and she was pulling me into her arms. She held me to her tightly, and I slipped my arms around her.

Burying my face in her neck, I inhaled her scent. An earthy tone mixed with my sister's own flowery perfume and filled my senses. She smelled like home, something I hoped to God I'd see again. Though with Ned still there, it wouldn't be a happy reunion. Not yet anyway. But that was a worry for another day.

"You be careful, okay?" Aeis said after a moment, holding me to her. "Don't do anything rash. You need to keep yourself and my nieces or nephews safe. I need someone to spoil when this is all over."

I chuckled and pushed back. "Well, you have to come back to be able to spoil anyone. So, you be careful too. Besides," I sighed and then gave her a teasing grin, "I think there are two guys who would be devastated to see you die."

Aeis ducked her head and sneaked a peek at the twins who were sharpening their blades a few yards away. "Yeah, well, we barely know each other."

I forced myself not to make a rude joke, but Raiden beat me to it.

"Never stopped them before," Raiden said, earning a glare from Aeis and a smack on the arm from me. "Hey, what was that for?" He rubbed his arm with a pitiful puppy dog look on his face.

"You know," I snapped before turning back to Aeis. I planned on reassuring her that the twins weren't like that, but the trumpets blared, signaling everyone to get ready.

My body tensed at the sound of them, the beat of my heart racing in my ears. I'd been in a lot of fights but never in a battle of this magnitude. Nervous didn't even begin to describe how I felt.

The guys seemed to freeze as well. Though they didn't seem as worried as I was. Their stances shifted as they prepared to take to the skies,

Firestar's wings came out first, and I knew my time with them was nearly up.

"Firestar." I grasped a hold of him before he could walk away. My eyes burned as I dragged him down, pressing a desperate kiss to his lips. I drew back with a deep breath, holding his face in my hands. I stared at him like I was memorizing every inch of his face, and in a way, I was. No matter what any of them said, there was a real chance none of them would come back.

"I know," Firestar answered my unasked question with a sad smile. "I know." He pressed his forehead against mine before releasing me to go to Jack.

Jack didn't kiss me right away. He cupped my face in his hands, doing pretty much exactly what I did to Firestar. His fingertips trailed along my cheeks and then traced my lips. Pale lashes fluttered close as he dipped down to give me a soft, gentle kiss. This time it was me who pulled back first. Jack's kiss made my heart hurt, and I couldn't take it.

I was thankful when Raiden pulled me into his arms. I was just this close to breaking down and bawling like a baby. Raiden's hand wrapped around my braid, angling my head back. His mouth ravished mine as he nipped and sucked at my lips. By the time he released me, I had forgotten all about my fear and wanted to pull the three of them into a tent to have one last hurrah.

The trumpets sounded again, and I had to let them go. Jack's wings sprouted from his back like a dance of snowflakes, they mesmerized me every time I saw them. Sadly, I didn't have time to get lost in them, because Raiden's bright electrified wings broke the air. He shot me a wink before flapping his wings and taking flight. Jack sighed and shook his head before following suit. Firestar was the last to go, his eyes lingering on me.

I gulped, my emotions getting the best of me, but before I could express them, Firestar was gone. They'd left me. They'd really left me here by myself. I forced myself to take slow, deep breaths, I didn't have time to freak out. A grand scale battle was about to go down, and I couldn't let my emotions distract anyone from the job at hand. I wouldn't be responsible for anyone getting killed.

I wouldn't.

"Are you doing all right?"

I jumped in place, spinning around to find Lord Amun standing behind me. He had donned his armor as well, the same suit he'd worn during the invasion of the unaligned camp. The concern on his face made him far less intimidating this time around though.

"No, not really." I glanced back to where the guys had taken off and sighed. "But I guess I don't have a choice. This must happen, whether I like it or not."

"I know the feeling." Lord Amun walked forward up the hill upon which we were supposed to wait and watch like helpless babes. I followed behind him, my eyes on the gathering troops below. "You wouldn't know it, but I hate fighting." Lord Amun's shoulders quivered, a wry grin on his lips. "I hate the sight of blood, and I'm a big baby when it comes to getting hurt."

I laughed politely. Whether or not what he was saying was true, I knew he was trying to help ease my nerves. No one wanted a stressed-out pregnant woman with magic powers.

"Firestar, however, he's like his mother." He glanced at me with raised brows. "Fierce, strong, and stubborn as an ox. Not surprisingly, there was never a fight she didn't win, except when it came to childbirth. That was one battle she hadn't been able to win."

The look of horror on my face must have been frightening because Lord Amun's expression dropped with his mouth, his hands waving in front of him. "Not that you will have that problem. You're going to be great. You have three powerful little guys - or girls - inside of you, I doubt they'd want anything to happen to their mother."

Trying really hard not to let his words freak me the fuck out, I decided to give my father-in-law a break. I placed my hand on his arm and offered him a small smile. "You're right. The chances of that happening are low. Plus, if any complications happen, I can always go to Earth. They have great doctors there, I mean, medics."

"Earth, huh?" Lord Amun sniffed. "I've never been. Maybe after all this, I'll take a little vacation there. Maybe you can show me around?" He arched a brow, and I couldn't help but laugh.

"Sure, it'd be my pleasure." Just as the words fell out of my mouth, a roar ripped through the sky. My eyes jerked to the battle below. Mouth dropping open and eyes wide, I watched as twin dragons, Raijin and Fujin, swooped through the sky. A bolt of lightning sprayed from their mouths and down on the fighters below.

The scent of blood filled the air as our men

poured into the field on both sides of Lady Nariko's mercenary army. I was sure some of those were men that used to be loyal to Lord Shen, but for all I cared, they could go sit on a lightning bolt and die.

The roars of the twins barely over shadowed the shouts and yells from down below. Some of the dragons actually used weapons while others lit up the battlefield with a full array of magic. There were entire swaths of ground that had iced over, proof that the ice dragons were doing their jobs. I just hoped it would be enough.

A few of the dragons had morphed into their half-dragon forms, their wings flapping in the air and causing large gusts of wind to blow in our direction. I was thankful to see that Raijin and Fujin were the only ones who were able to go full dragon. It gave us the advantage we direly needed. At least, that's what I thought until they started spraying their magic all over the field with no care as to where they were shooting their loads.

Fear that they might accidentally hit one of the guys, I searched for them in the crowd, but it was like picking a needle out of a haystack. They were several hundred yards away, and almost impossible to find. That was until a large group of men was thrown away by a swinging ice hammer.

Jack. My heart jumped into my throat. I took a hesitant step forward, but Lord Amun's hand stopped me. My gaze dipped down to it before going back to the battle.

Don't run out there, I had to tell myself. They're fine without you. You'll just distract them.

I kept repeating those words over and over like a mantra. Not that it helped much as every fiber of my being wanted to dart out there and find them. Help them before someone hurt them. The tingles in my stomach told me the babies wanted that as well.

A loud uproar jerked my attention back to the battle, where a whole section of dragons was thrown about, their bodies shaking from the electric bolts of Raiden's trident. Raiden moved so fast, he was like a blur, knocking men out of his way as he barreled toward the walls of his home. The only thing more magnificent to watch was the fight above.

Most of the fighters had chosen to stay on the ground. Fighting in the air was a challenge for most dragons, seasoned warriors or not. Of course, that's where I found Firestar. At least I was pretty sure I had. He was flying so swiftly that the only telltale sign of his passage were the screams and burning body parts falling from the sky as his kusarigamas sliced through the enemy.

I couldn't find my sister in the mix, though she didn't have a larger-than-life dragon form or a magical weapon to help me pick her out of the crowd. Knowing Aeis though, she was kicking ass and taking names.

Our father would be so proud.

Luckily, they were keeping the majority of the battle to the field, and we hadn't had to worry about any stragglers. I didn't expect that to last for long. We might have a lot of men, but someone always got through. Always.

The sound of my name being called was all the warning I had before I was shoved to the ground by Lord Amun. A bolt of lightning flew through the space where my head had been before. Lord Amun shifted to the side, so his weight wasn't on top of me, letting me sit up slowly, my eyes searching for the one who had cast the electricity.

A man wearing the bright yellow colors of the East came charging forward. Without even rising to my feet, my hand began to burn before a ball of fire shot out. It hit the man right in the chest, lighting him up like a Christmas tree. The man screamed and fell to the ground as another one took his place.

Jumping to my feet, I bumped Lord Amun with my foot. "Looks like we're going to get some action after all. Hope you skipped breakfast." I threw another fireball before shooting a terrified Lord Amun a grin. And they said I was the one with a weak stomach.

18

I didn't realize how much I needed to fight until those men started pouring over the ridge. It wasn't a huge amount, a dozen at most but enough to get my blood pumping, excitement in every movement.

Throwing fireballs left and right, I hardly had to think before the next one left my hand and blasted a soldier away. The others who had stayed behind to guard the border were swept up in their own battles. I couldn't take the time to glance back to see if anyone needed help, I had my own fight to focus on.

"You bitch!" a lightning dragon screamed at me as my fireball missed him, skimming his arm. Irritation filled me for missing, and only slightly for being called a bitch. Though I might be calling me the same if I were in his position.

But right now, it just made me dig my power into the earth, pulling up the vines to wrap around his legs, knocking him to the ground. He snarled and clawed at them, calling me even worse names than before. The more he struggled, the tighter the vines wrapped until they completely covered every inch of him.

"Call me bitch, will you?" I muttered, turning away from his still form in time to come face to face with another attacker. This one had half-shifted into his dragon form, his eyes yellow and slitted, and scales covered the majority of his face and arms. Before I could react, his claw lashed out and caught me across the shoulder and part of my chest.

Forcing myself to ignore the bloody wound, electricity crackled in my hand. With a growl, I shoved my fist into the guy just as his claw came down to take another chunk out of me. When my hand hit his chest, his entire body spasmed as lightning danced up and down his form, stopping his attack mid-strike.

His eyes rolled into the back of his head, his mouth foaming before he collapsed on the ground.

I bumped him with my boot, making sure he was actually out before turning back to the fight.

When no one immediately came at me, I took the time to scan the area. There were dozens of bodies littering the ground, but no more fighters coming our way. I searched for a familiar face in the swirling mass of the battle but couldn't find one.

Turning around in a circle, I kept looking this way and that, practically giving myself whiplash from how quickly I was turning my head. Where was Lord Amun? He'd been right beside me. Please don't be dead. Don't be dead. Raiden was already losing one of his parents in this whole debacle, I couldn't bear to see Firestar lose his father.

A hand clamped down on my shoulder, and on instinct, I commanded flames into my palm, a fireball ready to throw. My throwing arm relaxed as I turned around and found Lord Amun standing there with his hands up.

"Whoa, there," he cried. "I'm on your side."

I extinguished the fire and dropped my hand. "Sorry, I'm a bit jumpy."

"Understandably." Lord Amun nodded and then frowned, his eyes going to my shoulder. "You should have that taken care of."

Why was it that only when someone tells you

that you're injured, does it actually start to hurt? I'd barely remembered that I'd been cut before Lord Amun had so kindly reminded me. Now, it stung like a mother as blood dripped down, staining my shirt. The strap to my chest piece had been sliced through, leaving the top half hanging down.

Wincing, I started toward where we had the medic tent set up. I waved off the attendant as I entered, grabbing what I needed to clean up my shoulder. I hissed as the cleaning swab touched my heated skin. Holding it to the wound until the bleeding stopped, I took in slow, shallow breaths.

"You know you really should let the medic take care of that," Lord Amun gestured to where I had my hand pressed.

"It's not that bad," I insisted, pulling the gauze away to look at the wound. "See? Already stopped bleeding." Still hurt like a son of a bitch.

"You're almost as stubborn as my son." Lord Amun chuckled, running his hand through his red hair laced with gray. I had a feeling he'd have a few more gray hairs in there after this was all done and over.

"I'm not stubborn."

Lord Amun snorted. "Only someone stubborn would say that, and since you're pregnant three times over, your stubbornness meter is out of the roof."

I gave him an impatient look, not even bothering to comment on the pregnant jab. We were in a middle of a war, this wasn't the time to get into a petty fight. Even if he was being a jackass. And he said that I was the one like Firestar.

"So, what's the plan now?" I asked, fidgeting with my ripped strap. Eventually, I gave up and just let it hang there. This wasn't a beauty contest after all. At least, my guts weren't hanging out.

"The plan is to stay alive and stick to the original plan." Lord Amun leaned against the pole holding up the tent. "Our men are doing their job, and we are doing ours."

"But there's not any more coming this way." I gestured toward the hill where we still the enemy's bodies were still littered about. "You can't tell me you are happy just sitting here and waiting?"

"Yes, the hell I am," Lord Amun snapped, his eyes going hard and fierce. "My job is to keep this border clear and to—" He cut off his words, his mouth clipping closed.

My eyes narrowed at his slip up. "To what?"

"Nothing, just to keep this area covered." Lord

Amun crossed his arms over his chest. I didn't believe him for a second.

"Tell me what you meant." I stood to my feet, my gaze focused solely on him. Lord Amun shifted in place, my stare obviously making him uncomfortable. Good, I needed to practice my mom look. Three babies were going to be hard enough, but when they became teenagers? Hell, I didn't envy my future self.

Lord Amun scoffed and glared at the ground. "Damn it, I told them this wouldn't work."

"What? What wouldn't work?" I urged him on. I had a feeling I knew what he was going to say, but I needed to hear it from him.

He met my gaze and sighed. "They wanted me to make sure you didn't do anything stupid."

"Stupid?" My brows raised up into my hairline. "Like what?"

"Like going into the fight yourself." Lord Amun waved a hand toward the fight. "They know how you can get."

"And how's that?" I asked, my teeth gritting with my growing agitation. Lord Amun just stared at me as if too afraid to tell me what the guys had said. "Come on now, you've gotten this far. You might as well go all the way. What did those jerks tell you?"

"Goddamn it, I'm getting too old for this shit." Lord Amun cursed more than I'd ever heard any lord curse. Not that I should be surprised, he was Firestar's father. "They said, and this is a direct quote," - he shook a finger at me - "so don't go killing the messenger ..."

"I won't."

He sighed. "Make sure she keeps her sweet ass on this hill. Maya's not invincible. If she takes one step off this hill before it's over, I'll turn her over my knee faster than she can say sir."

I could tell Lord Amun was uncomfortable by the time he finished, and I tried to keep my annoyance out of my face, I really did, but it was hard to do when you're four months pregnant and the hormones are raging. He was lucky I didn't rip his head off.

My hands curled into fists, my anger pulsating through my veins. I knew it wasn't his fault. He didn't know - or maybe he did know, just a little - what those words would do to me.

I stomped away from him and toward the hill. The moment the fight was over, I was going to give those demanding jerks a piece of my mind. I could take care of myself. Hell, I was stronger than all three of them put together now that the babies were channeling through me.

My body hummed with energy as I glared down at the battle. It seemed to be winding down, and it took everything I had not to just barrel into the field. I wanted this to be over so I could bend someone else over my knee for once.

"Maya," Lord Amun stopped behind me but was smart enough not to touch me. Whatever he was going to say got cut off though. The gates around the city burst open and hundreds more soldiers came pouring out, fresh reinforcements to turn the tide of the battle.

That wasn't the worst of it though.

Coming out of the gates behind the men was a large dragon, dark blue with long thick spikes protruding out of its back. Its wings were made of water and were the most fascinating thing. I had never seen a water dragon before. I thought they were extinct, along with most everyone else.

"Is that …?" Lord Amun asked, just as in awe of the sight as me.

"Yeah, I think it is." I nodded and then something came to me. "Do you think that's the mysterious Drac we've heard so much about?"

"It'd be quite a coincidence if it wasn't." Lord Amun hummed. "I'd heard stories of him but had thought they were all rumors. You know, his men trying to make him seem more dangerous than he actually was." He scoffed and laughed. "I never expected to see a sea dragon in my life time."

I watched with growing anxiety as the dragon spewed water from his mouth with all the force of a giant firehose, knocking a whole line of our men back. He was a lot larger than the twins, so much so that when they came after him, one on each side, he didn't have to do much more than bat them away with his claws. The strike threw the pair across the field, slamming into the ground and taking several of our men with them.

"What the fuck?" I gaped as Drac turned our winning battle into a losing one. When I caught sight of a few familiar bodies heading toward the rampaging dragon, my heart skipped a panicked beat. I started forward unable to help myself as I watched first Firestar get tossed up into the air and then punted across the field. A small sound escaped my lips when Raiden was caught in his claws. My throat closed over as I watched him being squeezed tightly, at least until a crackle of lightning burst out of him, forcing Drac to drop him.

"Maya." I barely registered Lord Amun calling my name as my feet kept moving forward. My eyes were pinned on the dragon and the way he so easily tossed my guys like rag dolls. My pulse raced, and my body tingled with unreleased rage. Before Lord Amun could stop me, I was already down the hill.

My hands twitched, and my skin crawled. A low growl trickled out of my mouth as my body began to feel too small. My skin itched uncontrollably. There was too much anger, too much righteous need to hurt those who dared think they could attack my family, for me to think straight.

The last straw, the last damn straw was the sight of Jack being pinned down by Drac's powerful jaws. He was just about to snap down on him when suddenly he stopped. His nostrils flared, and his mouth fell open, dropping Jack to the ground, making my blood boil. His head jerked around, his eyes searching until they fell on something.

It took me a moment to realize what he was looking at. It was me. The air crackled around me as I moved through the field. Some of the Eastern soldiers came at me but were thrown back by the elemental energy building around me. The rest were smarter. They turned tail and ran the moment they saw their buddies getting hurt. I knew something was happening to me. Something big and unexplainable but I couldn't stop it. I didn't want to.

A dull ache started in my chest, but it wasn't painful. It was liberating, like I'd been locked up in a tiny room and finally had room to breathe. The fighting continued around me, but both armies gave me a wide birth. The ground shook with each step I took, and I glanced down to see the magnificent creature I'd transformed into, a full-blown dragon. My scales glittered an iridescent silver, but when the light touched them just right, a rainbow danced across the surface.

I'd never imagined I'd ever get to this level of power. I knew it was because of the babies. Without them or the guys to push me, I'd still be, well, a damn good fighter but never something as great as what I was now.

Just to prove how good it felt, I blew out a breath, and to my delight, a mixture of magic shot out of my mouth. Not fire, not ice, not even lightning, but a combination of the three and more. It was like all of the elements that had been building inside of me became one, and it was a powerful thing, so much more so than I'd ever felt before.

I didn't even bother to see the damage I had left

in my wake. I only had eyes for one dragon, and he was stomping toward me. I only had a moment to think, 'Oh fuck,' before he was on me. I bared my teeth, ready to rip into him, but he didn't attack. Instead, he stopped before me and sniffed.

He fucking sniffed me like he was about to try to mate me.

Here I was, trying to save the day, and this asshole thought he could just get a big old whiff of me and be all okay? I didn't think so. My claw swiped out at him in warning before he could try and get a closer sniff. Drac backed off and made a growl-like cough, his sharp teeth snarling at me.

I realized a split second later that he wasn't snarling. He was laughing. The mother f'er was laughing at me. This only made me let out a roaring growl in return, ready to beat the crap out of this guy who thought he could laugh at me.

Drac stared at me for a moment with his ocean blue eyes which only pissed me off even more. I jumped at him, my claws bared before me, but he sidestepped my charge, smacking me on the butt with his tail as he did so. A low growling laugh was the only response to my attack.

Whipping around, I slashed out with my tail, hitting him in the chest with a satisfying thud. He backed off for a moment before he shook his head and came at me. I prepared for his attack, expecting him to cut loose with his full power, but it was like he wasn't even trying to hurt me. Instead of tearing at me head-on, Drac ducked to the side and jumped at me.

A stinging pain burned into my throat as I realized he had clamped his teeth on the back of my neck. I thrashed around, trying to get him off me. He had a good hold on me though, and the rumble coming from his throat urged me to calm down and give up.

My eyes widened, and anger billowed up in me even fiercer than before. This bastard thought that he could top me! Like he could just make me submit with a few playful hits and a bite to the neck! That kind of shit might work with lions, but I was a dragon and I didn't submit to anyone.

I sunk to the ground, letting him think he had won, that I was submitting to his will. Really, I was just biding my time so that I could draw my power into a big ball, hidden from his view underneath me. There was only one way to get him off my back and end this now.

In one fluid movement, I jerked my head back and rolled the opposite way. The sudden twist pulled my neck free of his clamping hold, and before he could try and get me again, I released the incandescent ball of elemental energy. It tore through the air and straight into his chest, pushing him a few feet back. His claws dug into the ground as he tried to power through my attack, but he didn't have what I had.

Motivation and pregnancy hormones that refused to let me back down.

I poured more magic into my attack, my brows scrunching down in concentration as I tried to force a hole through this guy's chest. Sadly, I didn't get my wish, but I got a great consolation prize as Raiden's trident suddenly stabbed upward into the soft under skin of Drac's neck. Blood gushed out of his throat as Raiden twisted the prongs in the wound into him. A set of kusarigamas joined Raiden's initial thrust, followed by a swing of an icy hammer, all together sending Drac's head flying off his body and crashing to the ground in a bloody mess.

Once the rest of Drac's army saw his head and body in two different heaps on the ground, they began to lay down their weapons in surrender. Our men cheered even as they sent hesitant looks my way. There were three men though that weren't scared of me. No, they stared at me in wonder as they came toward me.

My jaw clipped closed as I breathed heavily through my nose. Jack was the first to reach me, his hand lifted to touch my muzzle. He had a studious look on his face, but even through that, there was a pinching at the side of his eyes.

"It's still me," I tried to say, but it came out in growls and snarls. Jack dropped his hand and stepped back. Oh, for Christ's sake.

I closed my eyes and focused on becoming myself again. My wings furled back into my back, my claws shortened, as did my snout. The tight feeling filled me again, and a sort of whoosh slipped over me until I was standing on my own two feet again. Sans clothes, apparently.

Immediately, Firestar unbuckled his breastplate and jerked the shirt he wore under it over his head. I took it from him and pulled it on. I couldn't even begin to think about where my clothes went in all this. Probably back on the hill, if they even survived the shift.

"Maya?" Jack asked quietly. "Are you alright?"

I wrapped my arms around myself and shivered. "Yeah, yeah. Freezing my ass off, but I'm fine."

"And the babies?" Firestar came over to me and pulled me into his arms, his inner warmth instantly heating me.

I focused on them for a moment, searching for some sign that they were alright. A series of bubbles responded. "Yeah, they're good. Probably should still get Tris to check me out though."

Raiden chuckled, wiping a trickle of blood off his face. "She's going to be pissed. But I have to say that was some badass shit. Did you know you could do that?"

"No," I shook my head. "And I don't want to do that again anytime soon."

"I wouldn't either." Jack stroked a hand down my back, his eyes not on me but on the headless corpse that had devolved from its dragon form. His eyes widened suddenly. "Wait, it's not over."

"What do you mean, it's not over?" I asked, frustration overriding my need for a nap. "The leader is dead. It would be stupid for his men to keep fighting now."

"No, he's not," Jack explained, grabbing me and pulling me toward the castle doors.

"Yes, he is," I argued, tugging at my arm. "His head is on the other side of the field. Not attached to his body. That is deader than dead can get."

"Not for a hydra." Jack looked over my head to meet Firestar's narrowed eyes.

"A hydra?" My head whipped back and forth between the two of them. "What's that?"

"A special kind of sea dragon," Jack explained, worry etching his face. Before he could explain more, the ground beneath us began to shake. I held onto him tight as I waited for it to stop. My eyes dragged over the wreckage around us. The other dragons had stopped fighting just after Drac had fallen, and now, most were trying to stay on their feet.

Something shifted out of the corner of my eye. My head jerked around to the body of the defeated sea dragon and my jaw dropped. What I thought had been a dead dragon was slowly getting to its feet. Without its head.

"How is this even possible?" I gasped as I stumbled back.

"A hydra can't be killed by cutting his head off," Firestar responded, his hand filling with fire. "If I'd known he was one, I would never have helped you cut it off."

"Why can't you cut its head off?" I stared up at the headless creature, completely dumbfounded by what was happening. I didn't remember anything about hydras. Sea dragons had gone extinct a long time ago, so for Drac to even exist was miraculous.

Curiosity and horror filled me as I watched the neck of the dragon move from side to side. The flesh where Drac had been decapitated shifted and moved as if there was something beneath the surface just fighting to get out.

"Quick!" I gestured toward it. "How do you kill a hydra?"

"Fire," Firestar said, the fireball in his hand growing to an even larger size. "Lots and lots of fire."

Just as he said that, the muscle and flesh broke away and two heads shot out from where only one had been before. My heart dropped to my stomach, fear coursing through my body. I'd already done my big magical gesture for the day, I wasn't sure I had it in me to do anymore. Especially not against an unbeatable dragon that now had two heads.

"Firestar …!" I said, anxiety lacing my voice.

"Don't worry," Firestar winked, and then gestured his head toward the rest of the fire dragons who had begun to create their own massive fireballs. "We've done this before."

"You have?" was what I wanted to ask, but I didn't get it out fast enough. Firestar made a sound that was a mixture of a roar and shout which the other fire dragons echoed. He did it two more times and I realized he was counting. The final roar was louder than the last, and on that cue, the collected fire dragon army threw their balls of fire at the same time.

The sky lit up as if a small sun had emerged. The sickening scent of burning flesh filled my nose, and through the light, I could see the barrage of flames hitting Drac. The soldiers had all aimed for his chest instead of his neck, his dark blue scales beginning to blacken and char.

At first, I thought they had got him. That it would be enough to incinerate him. But somehow, scales charred and flesh horribly burned, Drac kept coming, throwing his heads around like sledgehammers. Jack grabbed me and flew away from where Drac was aiming, landing so we stood by the castle walls.

"What are we going to do?" I gasped, clinging to him for dear life. "The fire's not working."

"Just wait," Jack said, his eyes intently watching Firestar and the other fire dragons. "Have some faith."

Faith? Who needed faith when you had raw power going for you?

I began to reach inside of me, looking for the magic that had let me change forms before, but Jack held me tightly to him. "Don't."

"But I did it once, I'm pretty sure I could do it again." I gestured toward the fire dragons barely making a dent in Drac's hide. "They're not going to win this way."

"Just wait. Please." Jack's eyes softened, the first sign of concern showing in his face.

Instead of arguing, I did as he asked and waited. And waited. Still, Drac kept coming, his own bursts of water being held back by judicious uses of fire magic, as the fire dragons kept out of the range of his two snapping heads. I was just about done with waiting when another roar filled the sky. My head jerked up to the sound as a large red dragon blocked out the sun.

"Who's that?" I asked in awe. The dragon was even bigger than Drac. When the sea dragon caught sight of him, he stopped trying to dodge the soldier's attacks and snapped at the sky.

Jack didn't answer me as the dragon flew across the sky and spewed fire on all of those below. Lightning and ice dragons scattered, none of them wanted to be caught in the thick burst of flame aimed for the sea dragon. I didn't blame them, I was happy to be far away from where his attack barreled through. I could feel the heat from here.

With the combination of the fire dragons on the ground and the larger one above, Drac didn't stand a chance. He yowled and hissed as he crumbled to the ground. His body burned to the bone, his scales falling off of him in chunks.

When he was nothing more than a pile of blackened meat, that was when they stopped. Nobody moved as we waited to see if the hydra was really dead. The ground shifted again, and I groaned in annoyance. "Not again."

"No, it's not. Look." Jack pointed toward the hydra where he had shrunk from his previous size. He kept shrinking down until he shifted back into his human form. He was as burnt as his dragon form, so much so that it barely looked recognizable as human. The only thing that made me believe it was him was the crisp hair on the top of what I could only assume was his head.

"Shit," I choked out. "That's just. Ugh."

"An understatement," Jack grunted and wrapped an arm around me, "but it had to be done."

I dragged my eyes away from the burnt mass and to where the full-grown fire dragon had landed.

His body shimmered and then he shifted down into a human form. That of a very naked Lord Amun.

Slapping a hand over my face, I buried my head in Jack's shoulder. "Tell me when it's over."

Jack chuckled and patted my head. "Such an innocent."

"Hardly," I snorted. "I just don't want to see my father-in-law naked."

"What's wrong with her?" Raiden asked, his foot steps moving close to us.

"I'm saving my eyes." I muttered into Jack's shoulder.

"Huh?"

"Lord Amun's state of undress is bothering her delicate sensibilities," Jack explained with a teasing tone.

Raiden chuckled. "Well, he's found some pants now, if that makes difference."

"Where'd he find those?" I asked, finally pulling my head back up. "I want pants."

"Off a corpse, I'd imagine," Firestar stated, his hand coming up behind me to pinch my bare ass.

"Hey," I warned and smacked his arm. "I can still shift again."

Firestar grinned, not at all ashamed of groping me in front of all these men.

"Man, I haven't shifted like that in, what?" Lord Amun mused as he approached us. "Ten years or so. Not since the last war. Now, I remember why." He rotated his shoulder and cracked his neck.

"Glad to see you still have it in you, old man." Firestar snickered, earning him a warning look from his father.

"So, did we win?" I asked, pulling away from Jack. "Is it over? Cause I'm starving."

Firestar's chest rumbled as he laughed and patted my back. "Yeah, I think we're good. Let's get you some food in you."

It was finally over.

Thank God.

I needed a cheeseburger and a nap. Maybe even a bath. Okay, totally a bath. Not in that particular order though. Oh, yeah, and pants. Pants were a must when storming a castle.

19

Unfortunately, I didn't get my pants first as I hoped. Also, my list expanded to add shoes to the top of it. Broken rubble was killer on the toes.

"Where to?" I asked as Firestar helped me through the wreckage of the Eastern capital. I could say one thing about Drac and his men. They were utter monsters.

The beautiful, lively marketplace I'd escaped through a few months back had none of the warmth or splendor to it. Stalls were smashed beyond repair. Houses were boarded up and their doors closed tight. As my eyes scanned the area, I would get glimpses of eyes peeking through cracks. The moment my eyes landed on them though, they disappeared, like rats scurrying back into their holes.

"What has she done to this place?" Raiden asked, sadness filling his voice. I wanted to wrap my arms around him and tell him everything would be alright. Which it would, eventually.

We'd won the war, but the battle was only half done. There was still Lady Nariko to deal with and then we had to find Lord Shen. Please, God, let him be alive.

Our steps were quiet as we filtered through the city. Our men did their jobs well, searching for any remaining soldiers loyal to Lady Nariko or Drac. They brought them out and tied them up, putting them with the rest of those who had surrendered. They would be a chance for those who were previously loyal to Lord Shen to repent for their crimes, but I couldn't say the same for Drac's men. They'd be dead before they even had a trial.

Such was the way of war.

Eventually, the doors of the homes began to open. Heads and fingers poked out of the entrances. They reminded me of turtles, coming out slowly and then darting back inside before finally emerging when they thought it was safe. A few of them recognized Raiden. Even more came out when the twins finally followed us in. I would have killed to known where they had found clothes after their shift.

"Praise be," a man cried out, coming up to Raiden. The citizen grabbed his prince's hand in his, shaking it enthusiastically. Raiden smiled politely, even though I'd have been ready to gnaw my own wrist off to get away from the guy. Irritable, who me?

Another half dozen people came out and did the same, each of them more excited than the next. A few even hugged Firestar and Jack, though the citizens seemed to think better of that after a moment. Thankfully, I was in the middle of the three and anyone who came too close received a warning growl from one of the guys. I guessed I wasn't the only one feeling a bit overprotective.

After what seemed like an eternity of picking through wreckage and greeting survivors, we finally reached the doors to the palace. For some reason, I imagined they would open on their own, a way to greet us for taking back the kingdom. Sadly, that didn't happen, and they sat there quietly, still closed tight.

"Are you ready?" Raijin asked Raiden, clapping

a hand on his shoulder. "There's no turning back now."

Raiden scoffed and pushed his brother's hand way. "Like that was ever a choice." He shook his head, a solemn expression on his face. "No, our mother put herself in this position. I won't feel guilty for this."

Lady Nariko waited up above. For judgment? For forgiveness? Or maybe even death? I wasn't sure, it wasn't my call. Really, it would be Lord Shen's decision, but first, we had to make sure he was still alive.

"Why don't we find your father?" I suggested, pushing through the wall of muscled flesh. "Or do you want to find your mother first? I've never been in this situation before."

Raiden snorted. "Think we have? We're just as clueless as you."

Fujin and Raijin stood in silence, a thoughtful expression on their faces. Eventually, it was Fujin who made the decision.

"We should go to Mother first. Who knows if she's even keeping our father in the dungeon anymore? For all we know, she's planning to use him as leverage."

"You think she'd be so ruthless?" Aeis gasped, appearing seemingly out of nowhere.

I hugged her tightly, having not seen her since before the battle. Pulling back, I gave her a once-over, but besides a few bruises and cuts, she was none worse for wear. "I see you're still alive."

Aeis snorted. "Those guys were barely a blip on my radar." She adjusted the armor on her shoulder. "Hardly worth my time."

The way the twins beamed at her even though we were about to take down their mother really said something about how much they cared for her. I wondered if she knew it too?

"Alright, let's save the war stories for after we take back the castle." Firestar raised a brow, and I shifted near him to loop my arm around his.

"Aye, aye, captain." I mock saluted him with the other hand, earning me an eye roll.

"Well, I guess there's no time like the present." Raiden took a deep breath and then pushed the front door open. We followed him, poised and ready for any attack that might be waiting for us in the castle.

The entryway was clear, but as we rounded the corner toward the throne room, a few stragglers of Nariko's army jumped out at us. Since Raiden and the twins were in front, they easily overtook them before the rest of us could even acknowledge we were under attack.

"Do you think that's the last of them?" I asked in a quiet voice. I wasn't sure I needed to whisper but better safe than sorry. For all we knew, the ones outside hadn't been the only ones Lady Nariko had at her disposal. I knew if it were me, I'd have a bunch more men in reserve to guard me.

As if I had just jinxed us, in front of the throne room door was a dozen or more men, all heavily armored and ready for battle. My hand warmed with fire as I prepared to get the first attack in, but Raiden grabbed my wrist before I could hurl the fireball.

"Wait," he whispered harshly, his eyes scanning the men, and then a broad smile spread across his lips. Raising his voice as he approached them, he said, "You're not going to guard anything with your asses to your enemies."

In one movement, the whole guard turned to Raiden. Their weapons lifted, and lightning crackled in their hands. That was until someone in their group called them off, and they lowered their weapons. A large, older man pushed through the group to greet Raiden.

"Well, better our asses than our honor." He smirked at Raiden before clasping hands with him and bringing him in for a chest-bump hug. The two began to talk in quick, low voices, though I could catch enough snippets to know this was talk of peace and not a plan as to how we would now kill each other like civilized people.

"So, what exactly is going on?" I asked aloud while we made our way over to them, the threat obviously over.

"Those," Raijin pointed out, with a gleeful look, "are our father's personal guard. They've been on the inside all along, biding their time until we were ready."

"And that man?" I cocked my head to the side. "Who's he?"

"Why, that's the captain of the guard, Gerald," Fujin answered this time. "He was like our cool uncle when we grew up."

"Oh, you grew up?" I smiled at them. "I couldn't tell."

Fujin threw an arm around my shoulder and laughed. "Out of all the women, my brother had to pick someone with a mouth like you."

I nudged him with my elbow and moved out of

his embrace. "If you think I'm bad, then my sister has really been on her best behavior."

Sidling up to Raiden, I bumped him with my shoulder as a reminder that we were still here. He glanced away from the older man and grinned as his arm wrapped around me, dragging me against his side.

"Gerald, this is the love of my life and mother of my future child, Maya Rose." There was so much love and pride in his eyes, it made my heart and face warm.

I ducked my head and greeted Gerald.

"Well, it's good to see someone was able to tame this wild child." Gerald chuckled. "Now, if only someone would do the same for your brothers." His gaze went over my shoulder to where the twins stood.

I grinned. "I don't think you have to worry about that." I glanced over my shoulder at my sister who was shamelessly flirting with the twins.

"I see that." Gerald's eyes slid away from them to me. "A family member of yours?"

"Sister, actually." I winked.

With another chuckle, Gerald shook his head. "Ah, to be young."

"I was just asking Gerald the situation in there,"

Raiden explained, pointing his thumb toward the throne room door.

"How's it going?" Firestar asked, having been unusually quiet for once. "Should we expect another fight?"

Gerald gave Firestar a curious look but shook his head. "No, we've secured the throne room. Lady Nariko is in there now with a few maids."

"And our father?" Fujin asked, his expression no longer laughing but anxious.

"He's still alive," Gerald assured him. "Your mother might be a piece of work, but I think some part of her still loves your father and didn't want to see him suffer. He had been moved to a room on the east wing and confined there, though we haven't checked for ourselves yet."

Raiden's arm tensed around me, and I knew he was holding back the need to run to his father's side and make sure he was alright. I wondered, if I was in his position, would I be so worried about my own father? My mother, sure, but my father hadn't done much to gain my love. Maybe with some grandchildren, he would loosen up some. One could only hope.

Without warning, Raiden released me and pushed through the group. He yanked open the throne room door and stormed in. The rest of us scurried to catch up, not wanting to miss a moment of the drama that was sure to unfold.

Lady Nariko sat on the throne, having a cup of tea like it was a Goddamn normal day in the palace. Did she not even care about the men outside dying for her? I asked myself once again how such a woman could have given birth to such remarkable, selfless men.

Her dark hair was pinned in a complicated updo that I couldn't even begin to figure out how to do myself, her dress a deep golden hue that I would never have worn, but somehow, she made it work for her. For all purposes, she looked like the queen she was pretending to be.

"My sons," she cooed when she saw us approaching. "So nice of you to visit. I was afraid you wouldn't come back."

"Cut the shit, mother," Raiden snapped as he barreled toward her like a train on a track.

Lady Nariko placed her hand on her chest and gasped. "Language, Raiden. I thought I raised you better than that." She sure had a knack for the dramatic.

"That was before you tried to whore out my mate," Raiden snarled, his anger pulsating through the room. "Before you decided your need for power was more important than your family and your people."

With a roll of her eyes, Lady Nariko sighed. "Don't be so dramatic, Raiden. I didn't choose power over you. I was trying to give you power. Power so you could be all that you could be and more."

Raiden let out a bitter chuckle. "I have power, mother. More than I will ever need, and it was no thanks to you."

"But what about your brothers?" she gestured to the twins waiting like silent volcanos just waiting for their turn to erupt. "Don't they deserve the same? Or would you be so selfish to keep something like her" - she gestured a hand toward me with a sneer - "all to yourself?"

"Don't talk to Maya that way," Raiden growled, stepping in front of me and blocking his mother from my view. "Never, ever talk to her again. This is the mother of my child, who could have been your grandchild, but now all she will be is a reminder of what you have lost … if you live that long."

"Would you kill your own mother?" Lady Nariko stared Raiden down, but he didn't flinch. When she realized she would get nowhere with him, she turned her words toward the twins. "Fujin, Raijin, you can't possibly agree with him. You're the heirs to the throne. You know the costs of ruling. We must think of the whole above ourselves. Is one little girl worth losing the power she could give you?"

Fujin crossed his arms over his chest. "That little girl just took out your friend, Drac. I wouldn't go talking like that about her if I were you."

"Unless you want a big hole in your throne room," Raijin added with a threatening growl.

Some would say that the twins were only standing up for me to earn points with my sister, but I wouldn't. I'd known from the beginning that these guys were good. Like breaking-your-heart good. There was nothing they'd do to hurt an innocent. Not that I was that innocent but still, they weren't like their mother.

"So, you're just going to kill me?" She shifted in her seat. For the first time, worry made her face look pinched. When no one immediately answered, she jumped to her feet. "You can't kill me. I'm the Lady of the East."

"Not anymore, you're not." Gerald stepped forward and gestured to a few other guards to grab her.

She struggled against him, screeching and yelling, "You can't do this. You obey my orders, not theirs. I am the Lady of the East."

"Nariko," Gerald's voice boomed through the throne room. "You are hereby under arrest for treason. You will be taken to the dungeon where you will await a trail ... if your husband is merciful enough to give you one."

A bitter part of me hoped Lord Shen wouldn't be merciful, but the part of me who didn't want Raiden and the twins to suffer any longer disagreed. I also tried to think about what I would do if I was in Lord Shen's position. If it were Firestar, Jack, or Raiden who had betrayed me. Could I kill them? My gaze moved over to them, and my heart ached.

It would kill a piece of me to hurt them. Even if they wanted me dead, I wasn't sure I could do it, and I prayed to God I never had to find out.

20

We waited in the throne room for the twins and some guards to bring Lord Shen back. They had already taken Lady Nariko down to the dungeon. Probably a good thing too, since my patience with her nasty words was being sorely tested.

They found Lord Shen exactly where Gerald had said he would be. He looked like he had aged thirty years since the last time I had seen him, but overall, he was in good health. I knew he was happy to see his sons at least.

I stood off the side as Lord Shen hugged each of his sons, one after the other. The reunion would have made the strongest of us tear up. Being that I was pregnant, I didn't even have a chance.

My sniffles drew Lord Shen's attention, and he walked toward me. "Look at you," Lord Shen grinned, urging me to hug him. "You've grown quite a bit since I last saw you. I hope you are taking good care of yourself." He held me tightly before patting my stomach.

I forced myself not to lash out at him. He's just been held prisoner for months, he could touch my stomach. Once. After that, it was hands-off. If I let it be known that it was okay to touch my belly, then everyone would take that as permission to rub it like I was some kind of dog begging for a scratch.

An arm came around my shoulders, pulling me away from Lord Shen. I glanced up at Raiden with a thankful expression. "Father, there's something I've been meaning to tell you."

Lord Shen's brows furrowed at his son's serious tone. "What's that? You're not splitting up, are you? Not with a baby on the way. What would people think?"

I resisted the urge to roll my eyes. And I thought Lady Nariko had been the dramatic one.

"No, no. Nothing like that." Raiden shook his head and waved a hand in front of him. He placed his hand on my stomach and smiled down at me.

"Maya isn't just having my child, she's having *our children.*"

We watched together in growing amusement as Lord Shen tried to process Raiden's words. It was easy to tell when he figured it out. His eyes widened, and a delighted grin covered his face, making him look younger than he had in a while.

"Children?" he asked, laughter in his voice. "As in more than one?"

"Three to be exact." Firestar moved in next to me and slid his arm around my waist.

"Wow, three." Lord Shen chuckled and glanced at the twins who were, as usual, with my sister, whispering amongst themselves. "I thought twins were bad. I can't imagine having three of those little hellions all at once."

Giggling, I placed my hand on top of Raiden's. "We'll manage. Besides, I have three wonderful fathers to help me."

"That you do," Jack agreed, moving in next to Firestar. "And we'll be here for you every step of the way."

"You better." I snorted. "You're the ones who put them in me, and if you think I'm hormonal now, just wait until my third trimester."

The look of utter mortification that covered all

three of their faces was worth every second of discomfort I was sure to have in the months to come.

"I remember your mother in her third trimester." Lord Shen grinned, a twinkle in his eyes. "She was a feisty one, but with all the griping and complaining came a lot of random needs for …" His voice trailed off with a wag of his eyebrows.

"Ew, come on." Raiden made a face. "I don't want to hear about you doing it with my mother." He smirked down at me. "Though I won't complain if Maya needs more physical attention." He leaned down and kissed me on the nose as I swatted at him.

"Sorry to interrupt the direction of this conversation — oh wait, no, I'm not." I gave Raiden a warning look. "But have you thought of what's going to happen now?"

Lord Shen's grin dropped, and I partly wished I hadn't said anything. He shifted in place uncomfortably before clearing his throat. "My wife had good intentions, even though they were executed completely wrong. But she's still my wife, and I love her, despite her actions."

"So, you're just going to let her go unpunished?" Raiden asked, the beginning of anger coloring his voice. I squeezed his hand, hoping to help him retain his temper. When it came to his mother, he was about as hot-headed as Firestar.

"Now, I'm not saying that." Lord Shen frowned and then stared down at the ground before lifting his gaze to Raiden's. "If you were in my position, would you be able to do it, to kill her? If it was Maya's life in the balance, instead of your mother's?"

"She'd never do that," Raiden immediately spat out. "She'd never try to use someone the way Mother tried to do to her."

"I think," Jack interrupted, interposing himself between the two before they could get into a shouting match, "what Lord Shen is saying is that it's not an easy decision. It never is when it comes to family."

"Exactly." Lord Shen gave a sad smile. "Your mother will be punished, but as to how? I have yet to let my heart close off enough to deal with her in a rational manner."

"Understandable." Jack nodded and then turned his gaze to Raiden, clearly expecting him to agree.

Raiden crossed his arms over his chest and glowered. "Fine."

Lord Shen seemed like he wanted to say more but thought better of it. Instead, he turned to me and asked, "What about you? Are you going to stay here in the East for a while?"

I frowned and glanced at my men. What were we going to do? We hadn't really thought about it with all that was still going on. There was really no point in going back North right now. We were only there until we could get enough men to save Lord Shen. Now that we'd done that, we really didn't have anything left to do.

"It's up to you, Maya," Firestar said, stroking a hand down my arm.

"Oh great, give the pregnant woman the hard decisions," I said bitterly and then dragged a hand through my hair. "Hell if I know where we'll go, but wherever we decide, it better be for a while." I rubbed my stomach and stared down at it with a loving look. "The babies and I are tired of jumping from place to place. I'd like to stay somewhere until the babies are born."

Jack hummed and then asked, "We could go back to the West? We haven't been there in a while, and I'm sure you'll want to be with your family when the babies are born."

I smiled at his consideration but said, "While I

would love to see my mother and have her to help me, I think you forget an important detail."

They were silent for a moment, and then Firestar growled, "Ned. That bastard is still out there waiting for his chance to take Maya out. We can't put her in that kind of danger."

"Hey," I said, poking a finger at his chest. "I can take care of myself. Or do I need to remind you of who exactly won this war." We grinned at each other until we realized we actually had to make a decision.

As luck would have it, my sister took a breath from the ocean that was the twins to put in her two cents. "I have an idea."

"What's that?" I put my hands on my hips, ready to hear whatever outrageous suggestion she had. My sister might be a great tactician and a better politician, but she still tended to go for the most extreme option first.

"Don't look at me that way," Aeis warned and crossed her arms under her chest. "It's a good idea. Really."

"Sure," I said slowly and then waved a hand at her. "Let's have it. What's your brilliant plan?"

Aeis grinned. "I never said it was brilliant." She tucked a lock of hair behind her ear and peeked back over her shoulder to where the twins stood. "Let me take care of Ned."

"No," I said firmly. "I won't put you in the way of that monster."

She sighed. "Look, you can't go because I won't let my nieces and nephews anywhere near him. He doesn't know that I know that he's a traitor. I can go back and keep an eye on him, and then, when the time is right, get rid of him." Aeis made a cutting sound as she slid her finger across her throat.

"I don't know." I shook my head. "I don't like you going at it alone. He's been able to hide who he truly is for this long. Who knows how evil he actually is?"

"Then we'll go with her." Fujin pushed his way into our little circle. "Let Raijin and me watch her back. Then you can rest your fears and focus on having those babies."

"Exactly," Raijin agreed, looking all too pleased with the prospect of being alone with my sister.

I wondered for a moment if they planned this all along. Though, even if they had, it was a good plan. Better than anything I'd have come up with. Plus, it took the responsibility of saving yet another kingdom out of my hands.

"Very well," I sighed reluctantly. "You can do it,

but the moment it becomes too much, you need to call for us. We have allies now."

"I know." Aeis nodded.

"And don't let Father in on what's going on," I continued with a warning look.

"I know," she growled, her eyes flashing with irritation, but I didn't let up.

"Because you know, he will think you're being paranoid. He'll get on his high horse and be all law-di-dah, I know what's best, go play with your dresses."

"Now, you're exaggerating." Aeis shook her head and started to walk away.

I chased after her, the guys chuckling behind me. "I'm serious, Aeis. This isn't like fighting on the battlefield. This is political warfare."

"I know!"

"I know you know, but seriously—"

"Maya!"

Hands grabbed me before I could continue my tirade, letting my sister get away. I growled and glared back at the hands holding me. I traced them up to Jack, a concern in his eyes. "What?" I asked him.

"Your sister gets the point, you should be thinking about getting checked out. You shifted into full dragon form, and most children don't survive through that." His hand stroked down my back as if to soothe me from an oncoming freak out.

I opened my mouth to tell him I'm fine, they're fine, but my vision clouded over and for a moment I couldn't breathe. A bright light filled my mind and at first, I thought I was going blind, but then something began to appear, another vision.

Three figures stood proud and tall on a balcony overlooking all of Waesigar. On one side was a pale haired man, his hair cut short, the bangs hanging over his face. His familiar face on a stranger's body told me that this was not any ordinary vision. The first man's veritable twin stood on the other side, but his hair was black and brushed his shoulders, a cheeky grin on his lips.

The one who stood out the most was the one standing between the two. Long curly red hair fell down the woman's back in waves, her eyes glittering emerald green as she glanced back at me. A smug grin greeted me as her mouth formed one word.

Mother.

"Maya," Jack's voice broke through the vision, bringing me back to the present. "Maya, are you okay?"

I shook my head and turned my head toward him. "I think I just saw our children."

"What?" Raiden rushed over to me, excitement in his eyes and the exact same cheeky grin that had been on the man's.

"What did they look like?" Firestar asked, a bit calmer than Raiden but not by much.

"A bit like us, actually. Or a combination of us." I shot Jack a smug grin. "But I think it's safe to say they're fine. Better than that, they're going to rule the world."

As the guys closed in around me, each other them chattering about what they hoped our children would be like, my heart warmed. The image of our children would keep me going for the years to come, and based on the grins I'd seen, I was going to need a crap ton of Advil – and dragon's tears. Lots and lots of dragon's tears.

THANK YOU FOR READING!

Curious about what happens next?

Find out soon in Dragons Unleashed!

AUTHOR'S NOTE

Dear reader, if you REALLY want to read the next Starcrossed Dragons novel- I've got a bit of bad news for you. Unfortunately, **Amazon will not tell you when the next comes out.**

You'll probably never know about my next books, and you'll be left wondering what happened to Maya and the gang. That's rather terrible.

There is good news though! There are three ways you can find out when the next book is published:

1) You join our mailing list by clicking here.

2) You can also follow Erin on her Facebook Page. We always announce new books in those places as well as interact with fans.

3) You follow us on Amazon. You can do this by going to the store page (or clicking this link) and clicking on the Follow button that is under the author picture on the left side.

If you follow me, Amazon will send you an email when I publish a book. You'll just have to make sure you check the emails they send.

Doing any of these, or all three for best results, will ensure you find out about my next book when it is published.

If you don't, Amazon will never tell you about my next release. Please take a few seconds to do one of these so that you'll be able to join Maya and the gang on their next adventure.